MR. JULY

Calendar Boys Series

NICOLE S. GOODIN

For all the babes born in July

CHAPTER ONE

Hudson

My gaze catches on the pink hair of the beautiful woman again, my arms raised in victory as I do a slow spin of the arena from the centre of the cage.

The crowd is normally nothing but a blur, but with a face like that, it's no wonder she stood out.

Everyone in the room is going crazy, screaming my name, stomping their feet against the hard floor and clapping their hands – celebrating the victory with me.

Considering I beat the shit out of other dudes for a living, I'm this place's golden boy.

I'm the crowd favourite here tonight, and with good reason. This is my home town now, and even though I was raised somewhere else entirely, they treat me like I'm the prodigal child returned – not to mention the fact that I've just won myself another title belt.

That makes two now.

Justin's hand lands heavily on my back, and I realise I'm frozen, still looking at the girl.

She's not even so much as glanced up at me. In fact, her eyes are on her feet, and she looks like she could hurl.

I don't know who she is, but given that she's got prime ringside tickets, she must be *someone*.

"Your uppercut needs work," Justin yells over the cheers of the crowd as I pull my eyes from the girl and turn to face him.

I flip him off. He might be my coach, but he's also my best mate.

"You're going to pull me up on my uppercut, when I just got us another belt?"

His face breaks into a grin. "Good things come in twos, baby."

"I've had a few knocks to the head." I chuckle. "But I'm pretty sure it's *bad* things and that they come in *threes*."

"Whatever, same difference." He throws his arm around my shoulder and shoves at my head, a shit-eating grin on his lips. "He messed up your pretty face this time."

I shove him back. "Fuck off."

He's right though. I can feel the blood trickling down my left eye and onto my cheek, plus my right eye is swelling so hard I can't see shit out of it anymore.

The calling of my name picks up, and I raise my hand to the crowd, my newly acquired belt strapped around my middle.

It doesn't feel too bad to be king of the ring, I can tell you that much.

"You done with this circus?" Justin asks, and I nod.

Fuck *yes,* I am.

Post-fight interviews are done – my opponent has already insisted on a rematch, even though I kicked his ass in only three rounds, but hell, if he wants to offer up his reputation for me to destroy further, then I'll take the pay day.

Winning is a high, but one that is wearing off fast.

This thing is done.

Justin throws my robe over my shoulders and gestures to the other guys that we're moving out.

Justin is my main trainer, but I've also got a couple of other guys. Randy is my grapple and floor expert and Owen works with me on conditioning and my leg work – kicks and knees. Between the three of them, they handle my management and nutrition – I like to keep my circle small.

We're exiting the opposite side of the cage from the girl with the pink hair, and I'd be lying if I said I wasn't disappointed about it.

No one catches my eye in a crowd on a normal day, and the fact that *she* did, has me curious – I want to know who she is and why she's here.

Justin leads me through the screaming crowd – security guards flanking us until we reach the hallway leading to the warm-up area and changing rooms.

I glance back over my shoulder, even though I know I won't see her.

I know I could ask Justin to go out there and invite her back here for me, but honestly, the pain is starting to kick in, and I'm not sure I could be charming even if I wanted to be – I certainly don't look my best.

I scowl and shrug my shoulders, which are starting to feel like lead, and try to relax.

There's so much lactic acid coursing through my body, and I know I'm going to be sore as shit tomorrow.

That bastard might have gone down like a sack of potatoes in the end, but he got a few good shots in along the way.

Randy jogs off ahead of me, to check on my ice bath I bet, and Owen sits an ice pack between my shoulders to try and give me some temporary relief.

The guys know me well by now, when I get this look on my face, it's time to get to work making me more comfortable.

"Anything you want the doctor to check?" Justin asks, his gaze travelling to my eyebrow.

"It'll need stitches or something," I tell him, I can feel the gaping cut across my brow, and it's definitely not going to heal up on its own.

"I'll see if he wants to glue it or sew it up." He nods.

We reach the door of my changing room; Owen tugs the robe from my shoulders and removes my belt.

I slide my shorts down my legs and limp towards the bath in only my boxer briefs.

"Might get him to check my leg too," I tell Justin.

He nods. "I'll get him to swing by in a few, I've gotta go grab my sister quickly."

I slide into the ice-cold water and wince. I'll never get used to this level of cold.

"Your sister?"

"Yeah, man, remember I told you she was finally back?"

I shake my head and try to relax my tense muscles.

"I told you yesterday she was coming to watch, I got her tickets..."

I shake my head again. He should know better than to talk to me about anything important in the lead up to a fight.

Most of the time I'm half-starved from trying to make weight, and almost delusional from all the training.

He shakes his head and chuckles. "We might get doc to check your head while we're at it... so, my *sister* – you *do* remember I have one of those, right?"

I flip him off again.

"Anyway, she's in the crowd and I've gotta go get her."

I wave him off with my hand and close my eyes, letting my head fall back against the rim of the bath.

I don't know how long I lie there for, but I hear Justin's voice coming back towards the room and I open my eyes.

There's still blood pouring out of my brow, so I hope he's got the doc with him; it's getting fucking irritating.

"I don't know, J, I'm not sure I should go in there," a female voice says.

"Don't be stupid, you're practically family."

His sister.

I've never met Ramsey, but it would seem I'm about to.

Excellent fucking timing.

Justin strides into the room, a grin on his face, and my eyes fall to the woman behind him... the one with the pink hair and the pretty face.

"Shit," I mutter under my breath.

She's *the* woman. The one from the crowd. The one who caught my eye and is now making my heart beat faster.

She's fucking gorgeous.

I'd need a cold shower if I wasn't already covered in ice.

"Ramsey, this is Hudson, but you can call him Horror if you want."

Her eyes find mine and she gasps, her face turns white and she sways on her feet.

"Oh fuck, I forgot about the blood," Justin hisses as he darts to catch her as she faints in his arms. "She can't stand the sight of blood." He groans as he scoops her up.

"Well, *shit*, I've never had a woman react quite like *that* to meeting me," I drawl, trying to cover the fact that I'm about two seconds away from leaping out of this bath to see if she's okay.

Justin carries her from the room, and it takes every last bit of my self-control to stay put.

CHAPTER TWO

Ramsey

"What the hell is wrong with you, Justin!" I shove his chest again, but it's no use, he's still in the shape of a professional fighter. "You know I can't deal with blood, shithead!"

He chuckles and ducks as I swing at his head his time. "Sorry, I forgot... *Jesus*, do you really think I did that on purpose?"

"I don't care if you did it on purpose or not!" I shriek. "I could seriously kill you right now."

"Take your best shot." He smirks arrogantly at me.

I groan in frustration. "That was so embarrassing, J, seriously, I just want to go home and never come back."

He chuckles again but tries to hide it when I glare at him.

"Don't sweat it, sis, Hudson is cool, he's not going to make fun of you, and he's had a few knocks tonight, so he's probably not feeling that sharp himself."

"Don't remind me." I shudder.

I don't know what possessed me to come to this fight. I can barely watch one on TV, let alone ringside, front and centre.

I've felt queasy all night.

He tugs me into his side and kisses the top of my head. "I'm sorry, Ramsey, seriously. I forgot about you and blood."

"It's like the most defining quality of my personality," I grumble.

"Maybe if you came home more often, I wouldn't have forgotten."

I narrow my eyes at him. He's always giving me a hard time for not spending more time around, but I'm here now – with no plans to go anywhere any time soon – unless he keeps subjecting me to bodily fluid and violence, in which case, I might just pack my bag and take off again.

"Can I go home now? I still feel like I could puke."

And die from embarrassment from fainting in front of the sexiest mixed martial arts fighter in the world – sure, I might not be able to stomach watching the fights, but that doesn't mean I don't know all their names and what they look like.

My family is MMA obsessed, and *I'm* obsessed with men so ripped they look like they're made out of stone.

Before they go and get all cut up and bloody at least.

"I want you to meet, Hudson." He tugs me in the direction of the door.

I dig my toes into the ground. I'm not going back in there until it's been declared a total blood-free zone, maybe not even then – seeing Hudson Scott in the flesh made me nervous.

Watching him dance around in the cage before the fight was like nothing I've ever seen before.

He's got this edge to him that's utterly frightening... a menacing look in his eye or something. He looks like a guy you do *not* want to fuck with, but beyond that, he's sexy as hell – body toned to perfection, handsome, chiselled features, sexy hair shaved close on the sides, and floppy on the top... and don't even get me started on that tattoo.

And he's my brother's best friend, which I'm sure means he's off limits, probably even for looking at.

I shove him away from me. "You go right ahead."

He chuckles. "Don't be a baby, the doc came out half an hour ago, he'll be good as new by now."

I want to ask if he'll still be shirtless, because I'm not sure I'll be able to hold a conversation if he is but decide better of it – the last thing I need is my big brother giving me shit for crushing on his friend.

This whole evening is the last thing I need if I'm honest.

I should have stayed home and watched a movie with Juliet.

She's going to have a field day when she finds out I fainted in front of Hudson 'The Horror' Scott.

She might prefer to read a book than watch sport, but that hasn't stopped her from perving on every inch of the man on the other side of this wall.

"Go check," I tell Justin.

He shakes his head at me but does as I tell him.

I don't know why I'm stalling, but my belly is fluttering with nerves that have nothing to do with my hatred of blood.

"All clear, Ram-Ram, move your ass."

"Don't call me that," I hiss as he snags my arm and drags me into the room.

The bath is empty now, thank god, because even all banged up, his body was a fine sight soaking wet – it's the only reason I didn't notice his face right away.

"Horror, this is my sister..." he calls, and my eyes skim the room, finding the man he's speaking to sitting in a chair, one of his legs resting on another chair in front of him. One of his eyes is swollen shut and I can see bruises forming on his jaw.

Hudson raises his head, first looking at my brother and then at me.

One side of his mouth turns up slightly, but he doesn't say a word.

I raise my hand in an awkward wave. "Hey."

"Hey," he replies.

"Don't both talk at once," Justin drawls as he drops into a chair next to Hudson.

He shoves one in my direction and I slide into it.

"Uh, I'm Ramsey... sorry about the fainting."

I glance quickly up to his brow, and thankfully, it's all patched up now and covered by a crisp white bandage.

He's wearing a shirt too – another win, because I'd hate to get caught drooling.

He smirks and then winces at the movement. "Hudson," he introduces himself. "And it's no worries."

I divert my eyes to the messy pile of hand wraps at his feet.

"Did you enjoy the fight?" he asks, and I look up in surprise.

His voice is smooth, like a good whiskey going down.

I scrunch up my nose. "Umm... *sure...*"

"You don't sound very convinced."

"I can't really watch," I admit. "The sound of bone hitting bone... the blood..."

"She was probably trying not to puke her guts out the whole time," Justin tells him, and I want to smack my brother again. I do *not* want Hudson Scott thinking about vomit and me in the same sentence.

He eyes me curiously – with the one eye that's not swollen shut anyway. "Why'd you come to watch the most brutal fighting there is if you can't stomach it?"

I point at Justin. "He doesn't know what the word 'no' means."

Hudson's lip lifts again, just a little. "I've never known him to be good at listening."

These two men have been friends for about four years, and maybe I am a shitty little sister, given that this is the first time we're meeting.

Justin nearly made it as a pro fighter a few years ago – that's how he and Hudson met, but a career-ending injury took my brother out – which I wasn't exactly gutted about if I'm being honest – so he's been training and coaching the rising star in front of me ever since.

At least now when Justin sets foot inside a cage, it's purely for training purposes.

Hudson raises his arm, and just when I think he's doing some type of stretch, his hand darts out as fast as lightening and smacks Justin around the back of the head.

"Ouch, what the fuck?" Justin growls at him.

"That's for making your sister sit through something she hates."

I try but fail to cover my grin. "It wasn't all bad," I admit as I think about getting to watch Hudson twist and turn as he threw practice punches at the air in front of him.

Justin raises his brow at me in question, and I shake my head. "Never mind."

Hudson is still watching me, and it's beginning to make me nervous.

"Are you carrying any injuries?" I ask, trying desperately to distract myself from his intense stare.

He points to his face.

"Anything less obvious?" I say with a roll of my eyes.

"My leg." He tips his head towards the leg he has propped up on the chair. "I thought it was just from throwing kicks, but I think there might be some damage to the calf muscle... why? Do you like seeing me in pain?" He smirks.

I let my eyes trail over his lean leg. "I'm a physio," I explain, "so call it a morbid curiosity... I treated a few fighters while I studied."

"You should go see Ramsey in a few days." Justin smacks Hudson's arm excitedly, like he's a genius for coming up with the idea.

"I'm sure he already has someone more qualified than me to take care of that," I reply quickly.

"Nah, the guy we have is shit, right, H?"

I let my eyes wander back to the man in question. "He's actually terrible... would you mind?" His dark menacing stare is hard on me, weighing me down, and I don't know how I could say anything but yes. So I do.

God help me.

I'm going to have to lay hands on this scary, sexy man and be required to remain professional while doing it.

Yup, Juliet is going to have a field day with this.

CHAPTER THREE

Hudson

This was a bad fucking idea.

A *really* bad idea.

I might look like one hell of a tough bastard, and don't get me wrong, in the cage, I *am*, but just the thought of letting my best friend's little sister put her hands on my body is making me break out in a sweat.

"What's up with you? You're jumpy as shit." Justin scowls at me as he drives me across town to the house Ramsey is sharing with one of her friends.

I shake my head in reply.

"Those ribs giving you grief?"

I'm pretty sure one of them is cracked, but that's nothing I haven't dealt with before and won't deal with again. A couple of dodgy ribs is the least of my worries.

Injuries like these are the reason I only fight a couple of times a year – I make enough money from the fights I do take to be able to afford my body that luxury. Because of that, getting hurt is no big deal – I've got time to recover.

I don't think I could fight every couple of months like I did when I was twenty. My twenty-seven-year-old body doesn't take a beating quite the same way it used to.

"It'll be right."

"We'll have Ramsey strap it nice and tight."

I nod. "Sure."

Fuck.

That's the very reason I hadn't mentioned it. I don't know how I'm meant to handle her fingers touching my leg, let alone my chest.

If Justin knew the thoughts I was having about his sister and her sexy ass, I'd be a dead man – regardless of how many title belts I might hold, I don't think a fighter in the world could stop J from defending her honour.

"We need to get you right so we can get back in the ring, work on your striking."

I glance at the window as he turns down a quiet street.

"I'm on break, you mad fucker."

He chuckles and pulls up outside a small, white weatherboard house.

"No rest for the wicked, Horror, you should know that."

He jumps out of the car and comes around to my side to help me get out.

I really should be using crutches, but I've always been one to take medical advice with a grain of salt, so I'll limp instead.

"She's working from home?" I question as we approach the front door.

"Yeah, she's got a massage table set up in the front room."

"So she's staying put then?" I ask casually. "Not taking off again?"

"Yeah..." He raises his brows. "She's here to stay... what's with the sudden interest in my sister?"

I clear my throat as he knocks on the door.

It could be because she's beautiful, or because she set me on fire with just a look... or it could be because I'm imagining her hands on my body in ways that have nothing to do with fight injuries.

His eyes narrow as though he can read my thoughts.

"She's your sister." I shrug. "You're always going on about her..."

His eyes narrow further. He's not buying it.

"If you're thinking about Ramsey in *any* way that isn't like a little sister, then you better shut that shit down, *right now*... you're like a brother to me and—"

"Hey!" Ramsey swings the door open and cuts off her brother's threat.

"Ramsey, hey," I offer with a wince.

She's wearing the shortest shorts known to man, and it's going to be a problem.

"Hey, sis." Justin leans in and kisses her forehead.

I wonder to myself what I'd have to do to get my lips on her soft skin, before mentally giving myself an uppercut – as shitty as Justin tells me it is.

This girl is off limits.

End of fucking story – and the sooner I figure that out, the better.

"You look like shit." She raises a brow at me. "We better get you checked out."

"Tell me what you really think." I grin at her.

She points to the closest door to us, off the hallway.

"His ribs are giving him trouble, don't let him tell you otherwise," Justin says as he strolls down the hallway, away from the room I'm going to go into. All alone. With his sister.

"Don't eat all my food," Ramsey yells after him. "Come on in." She holds the door open for me and I hobble in. "That doesn't look good." She frowns.

"Kinda comes with the territory, I'm afraid."

She pats the side of the bed and offers her arm to help me scoot onto it.

"Never been able to figure out why anyone wants to be a punching bag for a living, but hey." She smirks as she picks up a clipboard from the desk in the corner.

"You're a lot more confident when I'm not bleeding," I inform her.

She laughs lightly. "You just keep your blood *inside* your body, and we'll be fine, you and I."

You and I. I like the sound of that.

Shit, I can't think like that.

Maybe we could be friends. I could deal with spending time with a woman like Ramsey.

"So, what are we looking at here?" she questions. "The calf, ribs... anything else?"

"My neck hasn't been feeling the best and I think I might have sprained my ankle as well."

She scribbles down what I'm saying onto the sheet of paper. "Okay... nothing like injuries spanning the *entire* length of your body."

"Never been one to do things by halves." I smirk.

She shakes her head, a small smile playing on the corner of her lips.

She sets down the clipboard and crosses the room to close the door.

I watch her every movement like a hawk.

"Let's get your shirt off," she instructs, and I swear I hear a slight tremor in her voice.

"I might need a hand."

She nods and moves towards me from the spot she was lingering in by the door.

It's as though she's afraid to get too close to me.

I can't say I exactly blame her – I do scary well.

She stops directly in front of me, my legs splayed wide so she can stand in between.

She reaches for the hem of my shirt and slowly drags it upwards, being careful not to touch me.

"Lift," she instructs.

I lift my arm on my good side and she slides the shirt up, over my head and back down on my bad side until I'm half naked in front of her.

"Alright then," she breathes, her eyes raking over my torso.

I should know better, she's only doing her job, but when her eyes linger on my skin, I *feel* it.

She leans in, her thigh brushing my knee as she glances at the side of my neck.

Our faces are so close, if I were to turn my head my lips would brush hers.

I can smell nothing but her sweet floral scent, and my head is swimming.

"Any pain down your shoulders or back?" she asks, and I'm reminded that this *isn't* an intimate moment; this is recovery – *rehab* – with a woman I'll never be allowed to touch.

"Not at the moment," I reply, my voice hoarse.

"Good," she says as she steps back a little bit, giving me space to clear my head.

"I think we should get these ribs taped up first and then we'll move onto your neck and then the rest of you, alright?"

I nod.

She turns and grabs some tape from her desk.

"Sitting up nice and straight," she instructs as she rips a length of blue tape from the roll.

I do as I'm told.

"Breathe in."

She runs her hand ever so gently across my abdomen, and I feel goose bumps breaking out in its wake.

She stretches the tape across my black and blue rib cage and sticks it down tight.

It hurts like hell, but I know it'll feel better once she's done.

She repeats the action until she's satisfied that I'm held together firmly.

"How does that feel?" she asks softly.

She's back standing between my legs – in a position that is far too tempting to wrap her in my arms and kiss her.

I twist gently, testing it. "Better." I nod. "Thanks."

She smiles. "Do you think you can lie face down?"

I eventually get settled on the bed, and her hands start kneading and massaging at my neck, and the entire time I have to lie to my dick and pretend that she's Bruce, the overweight man that usually takes care of my injuries.

***

"Did you make him cry?" Justin asks as Ramsey helps me down to the living room.

He's laxed on the couch, his feet on the coffee table and his arm slung over the back of the couch. Next to him is a sweet-looking brunette girl.

"Get your feet *off* my coffee table and your arm away from my friend, you little skeeze," Ramsey fires at her brother.

Justin just chuckles. The girl blushes.

"Hudson, this is my flat mate Juliet, Juliet – Hudson."

She gestures between the two of us.

"Nice to meet you, Juliet."

She blushes deeper. "It's *so* good to meet you."

She kicks at her brother's feet and pushes past him.

He scowls as he loses his footstool.

"Juliet is a big fan." Ramsey sniggers as she helps me lower into a chair.

"Oh yeah? You like watching the fights?" I question her as I watch Ramsey disappear into the kitchen out of the corner of my eye.

Juliet shakes her head, and before she gets a chance to explain, Ramsey calls out. "She's a fan of your abs, champ, not your fight record."

"Oh my god, make her stop." Juliet groans and covers her face.

Justin chuckles and drops his arm from the back of the couch, onto her shoulder. He drags her into his body, and she buries her face in his chest.

He strokes her hair, a huge grin on his face. "Don't sweat it, Juliet, Romeo's got you."

I roll my eyes at him.

Ramsey appears in the living room again, and my focus instantly shifts to her.

"Get your filthy little paws, *off* of her," she demands, scowling at her brother as she does.

Juliet giggles and attempts to wiggle free of Justin, but he isn't having it.

"Fair's, fair, sis, you just had your hands all over my best mate, so I'm returning the favour."

"You're an idiot," she retorts, but I don't miss the slight pinking of her cheeks.

"How's the battle wounds?" Justin asks me, his arm still firmly around the woman next to him.

"She didn't make me cry, but it was fucking touch and go for a few minutes there."

"I'm going to need to see him back, at least twice a week for a while yet."

What a damn shame that is.

"I'm not his keeper, what are you telling me for?" Justin frowns at her.

"You're his coach, aren't you?" she demands.

"You realise I'm right here?" I raise my brows at the two of them. "And I'll be here," I promise, Ramsey, "whenever you want me."

She smiles wide.

"Maybe I'll tag along after all," Justin grumbles to himself.

Ramsey narrows her eyes at him.

He doesn't notice. "What are you girls doing on Friday night? We're going to a party."

"Good for you," Ramsey quips.

"I thought you might want to come, smart ass."

"Then why don't you say, 'We're going to a party Friday night, do you girls want to come'?" She slides onto the couch next to me and tucks her legs under her body.

I'm hyper aware of her now, ever since her hands touched my skin.

I'm drawn to her in a way that makes no sense to me.

"That's what I said," Justin argues.

"No—"

"You two make me so happy to be an only child," Juliet interrupts Ramsey and Hudson's argument. "Seriously, do you have to fight about everything?"

I chuckle.

"*Fine.*" Justin runs his hand through his hair in exasperation. "*Do you* want to come with us to the party on Friday?"

I don't know whether I want her to say yes or no.

On the one hand, I hope she comes, so I can get to know her better, but on the other, I'm not sure I can handle knowing more – I'm already teetering on a thin line.

This attraction is purely physical right now, and I'm in control of myself – physically at least. If my head and my heart get involved, I'm not sure I'll have the self-control to stop.

"Depends who's going to be there." She smirks.

"*I'm* going to be there. That's all you need to know."

"Will there be any hot guys?" Juliet questions.

Justin looks between her, his sister, and me.

"No," we both growl in unison, for different reasons, I'm sure.

The girls giggle and look at each other – some type of silent conversation goes down and Ramsey pops a shoulder. "I guess we could make an appearance."

"Good. You've missed out on three years of partying with me."

"That's probably a good thing, J, I've seen the way you party," she says, her tone wary.

He chuckles. "Horror here throws the best parties, so we'll show you a good time."

I watch Ramsey's gaze shift to me. "It's *your* party?"

I shrug. "Yeah... everyone expects a victory party."

Juliet says something to Justin, but I don't catch it; I'm too busy staring at his sister.

"You sure you don't mind if we crash?"

"Come," I insist.

"It was his idea to invite you, Ram-Ram."

"Don't call me that. I'm not a sheep," she scolds him, without looking in his direction.

I hear him chuckle.

"You're always welcome," I reassure her.

"Told you, sis, you two are like family now."

"Yeah," I say with a frown, "*family*..."

CHAPTER FOUR

Ramsey

"Oh my god, spill! Is he as ripped as he looks?" Juliet cries as she bounces up and down excitedly on the couch. "I can't believe 'The Horror' was just in my living room. Most people shit the bed when they get a look at your brother up close, but *Hudson Scott* is on a whole-nother level – no offence."

I shake my head in amusement and tuck my feet back up under my butt.

He's on another level alright. A really fucking dangerous one.

Everything about the man screams trouble, yet my entire body keeps telling me to get closer.

I never have known what was good for me.

"He's even *more* ripped." I sigh and drag my hand over my face. "Seriously, it's like he's made from solid granite. The abs on him... they'd be enough to have male models everywhere weeping."

"Remind me again why I didn't study to be a physio?"

"Because you like animals more than people."

"This is a valid point." She nods in agreement. "But I think I could grow to like people more if they all looked like the two that just walked out our door."

I groan. "Don't talk about my brother, that's gross."

She rolls her eyes. "Fine, but me keeping quiet isn't going to make him any less hot."

I ignore her, my mind drifting back to the way Hudson told me to come to his party. He seemed genuine, like he really wanted me to be there.

"So... this party, it's going to be full of sexy fighters and bitchy girls, right?"

"Without a doubt." I sigh.

I'm not so sure about it now that Hudson isn't here to make me feel welcome.

The fight scene isn't one I feel comfortable in – in fact it's a big part of the reason I chose to go to school on the other side of the country.

Everyone here knows who my brother is, and my father too – or more to the point, who he was in his day.

There's a whole room in my parent's house dedicated purely to my dad's sporting achievements. He was a king in the sport of mixed martial arts.

He works for the UFC now and owns a fighter gym, so if anything, he's *more* passionate about the sport now than he was when he was the one in the cage.

Justin's shoulder injury devastated him, almost as much as having a daughter who can't stomach watching two people throw punches.

I've always felt like a disappointment in my father's eyes – to the point where I barely speak to the man.

I talk to Mum a couple of times a week, but I've only seen her in person once since I moved back to my home town a month ago.

She's a strange woman, my mother. She lives in my dad's shadow – if I didn't know better, I'd say she had battered wife syndrome – but I know my dad would never lay a finger on her.

I think he's just spent so long protecting her that she doesn't have a clue how to protect herself.

"We're really going to go?" Juliet asks.

"We're going." I nod. "Justin won't let us out of it now."

"I'm going to have to borrow something hot to wear."

"If you're dressing up to impress my brother, I will seriously puke."

She blushes but shakes her head. "Hot fighters, remember?"

I shake my head at her. There's only one guy she's got her eye on, as gross as the idea may be to me.

I just don't want her getting her hopes up when it comes to Justin. He's not exactly known for settling down and he's always said that Juliet is like a sister to him.

The same way I am to Hudson, apparently.

I frown at the way he said the word 'family' earlier.

I don't want to be his family.

I let my head fall back in frustration. I shouldn't want to be his *anything*.

Hudson Scott is dangerous, and in a way that has nothing to do with his performance in the cage. I'd do well to remember that.

***

"Ramsey!" Juliet shrieks from her room.

I drop my can of hair spray and rush from my room, down the hallway and into her bedroom.

"What's wrong?"

She wobbles on the heels she borrowed from my closet earlier today to wear to the party tonight.

"How on earth do you walk in these things? I feel like a newborn giraffe." She yelps as she tries to take a couple of steps.

I snigger as her arms flail around at her sides.

She reaches for her bed and dives onto it.

"You just walk." I shrug.

She twists around and glances at the high-heeled ankle boots I'm wearing.

"You ran down here in those?"

"Yup," I reply as I drop into her clothes-covered chair.

"I *hate* you." She pouts.

Her eyes move up my legs as she appraises my outfit.

"Dammmmnnn, girl. The scary fighter might eat you for a snack."

I roll my eyes. "I'm not trying to impress Hudson."

She tugs at the buckle near her ankle that's holding her shoe on. "Sure, sure, and I walk like a supermodel on a catwalk in these things," she replies sarcastically.

"Seriously, I'm *not*," I insist.

Lie.

"I haven't even thought about him since the other night."

Lie.

"I'm just going to see Justin."

Another lie.

"You keep spewing those lies, and maybe you'll even start to believe them." She giggles as she throws the heels onto her bed. "Now, let's find me some shoes that won't break my neck."

I shake my head in amusement and reach for a pair of flats from her floor. I toss them to her, and she smiles gratefully before sliding them on her feet.

"The cab is going to be here in five," I tell her as I get to my feet, smoothing down my short black dress as I do.

I turn to walk back out of her door. "Serious, Ramsey, you look smokin', he's going to shit himself when he sees you."

I consider arguing the point with her, but truthfully, I can't be bothered – this outfit, hair and makeup might not have been done specifically for him, but I certainly had him in mind – the same way I have ever since he walked out my door.

I don't know what it is about him – obviously he's sexy as hell, but I've seen plenty of good-looking men in my life. This is more than that. I'm drawn to him, even when I know I shouldn't be.

I grab my small bag from the hallway table and glance in the mirror at my pink hair, curled into loose waves around my face.

My hazel eyes are framed with thick, dark lashes thanks to my new mascara and my lips are a deep pink.

"C'mon, Jules!" I yell at the same moment a horn sounds from outside our place. "Cab's here."

She comes flying out of her bedroom, much more stable on her feet this time, slinging her bag over her shoulder.

"I'm ready."

"Careful, girl, anyone would think you were excited."

She pokes her tongue out at me. "You keep my dirty little secrets, and I'll keep yours." She giggles.

CHAPTER FIVE

Hudson

I glance at the watch on my wrist and then at the door again.

"Who are you waiting on? You invite a chick or something?" Justin asks, his brows raised as he follows my line of sight to the still-vacant doorway.

I shake my head. "Nah, just wondering when Rusty and Beast are gonna rock up."

He nods. Justin never has been the best at knowing when I'm lying through my teeth.

"Rusty is always late." He takes a swig of his beer and slides his phone out of his pocket. "Speaking of late, I don't know where the fuck Ramsey is."

"I forgot she was coming," I reply as I lazily glance around my packed living room.

There's a shit load of people here, none of which are particularly interesting to me. Next to none that I'd actually consider to be more than an acquaintance.

That's the thing with having such a high-profile sporting career – people think they know you.

People don't know shit about me.

I pretend I don't notice him watching me.

He's been down my throat about Ramsey for the past two days, drumming it into me that I've somehow taken on the role of her surrogate big brother – apparently it's my duty to look out for her now too, and 'looking out for her' means keeping members of the opposite sex away from her, in Justin speak.

He sure as fuck is protective of his sister.

I take another drink of my beer, draining the bottle this time.

I'm reaching for another one when he says the words I've been dying to hear for the past hour and a half. "Here she is."

My eyes snap up to the door, my beer forgotten.

Justin is already moving across my living room, towards her.

I swallow deeply. *Jesus Christ*. Why'd she have to come here looking like that?

She's not the innocent-looking baby sister J talked about when he described Ramsey. Not even close.

Fuck, she's beautiful, sexy, and *tempting*.

Her smiling face is all I see as I move towards them, following the path Justin took.

"About time you showed up, I thought you were going to stand me up." I hear Justin say as he releases Ramsey and picks up Juliet.

"Babe, you look good enough to eat," he says as he lifts her clean off her feet and into his embrace.

I swear he loves that girl. I know he likes to drive Ramsey insane more than anything, but I don't think it's all an act. He's got a soft spot for his sister's house mate.

"Um ew. I don't want to hear those words come out of your mouth *ever* again," Ramsey hisses.

"Hey, pinky," I say, and she freezes, her hands dropping from where she's placed them on her hips.

She slowly turns to face me, and that lump is right back there in my throat again.

"Hey, champ," she replies, her voice a hoarse whisper.

I smirk. I like the way 'champ' sounds coming from her mouth.

Justin puts down Juliet and whispers something in her ear that makes her blush.

I don't do a thing but look – at Ramsey.

"You sure know how to throw a party."

I glance over my shoulder at the people filling my home. "I guess."

"Your house is really nice."

"You'll have to come back one day when it's not so crowded."

"I will?" she asks quietly as Justin and Juliet step closer.

"I won't take no for an answer."

She dips her head, my intense stare too much for her.

"You girls want a beer?" Justin asks as he slings his arms over both of their shoulders.

"Look at that, you know how to ask a question after all," Ramsey muses.

I chuckle as he glares at anyone that is in his way of getting back to the kitchen.

The crowd parts for him, and I gesture for them to go ahead.

Justin might not fight anymore, but he's earnt the respect of everybody in the industry.

I follow behind the three of them.

I don't mind the view from the back.

I let my eye slide up Ramsey's lean legs to the bottom of her dress.

Nope, I don't mind this view at all.

Justin drops his arms and goes to grab something from the fridge. I flip the lid off another beer and bring it to my lips. I need something to take the edge off.

"Wine?" Justin asks as he waves a bottle in the girls' direction.

"Me please." Juliet grins.

"I'm good," Ramsey replies.

I eye her curiously and hold out my beer.

She takes it, her eyes never leaving mine as she brings the neck of it to her lips and drinks deeply.

Jesus, what I wouldn't give to be that bottle.

"Since when do you drink beer?" Justin demands.

"Since always." Ramsey looks away, and I mentally give myself a knee to the guts.

I need to get my shit together before I wind up a dead man.

I grab another beer and down half the bottle in one go.

I've barely drunk in months – fight prep and all, so this is going down a little too well.

"So, what now, champ? What happens at one of your parties?"

"There's a band in the back yard."

She shakes her head. "I don't feel like dancing."

"Well I do." Juliet grabs Justin's hand and drags him out of the kitchen, in the direction of the sliding door that leads out back.

Justin shoots me a look over his shoulder and points to Ramsey. It's awfully fucking clear that I'm in charge of protecting her for now.

Too bad that the very thing she'll need protection from, is me.

"So..." Ramsey says as she leans her elbows against the bench. "This house is a *mansion*, exactly how loaded are you?"

I chuckle. "Loaded enough."

She giggles and her eyes roam the room, looking at the groups of people talking and laughing.

I stroll around the bench until I'm next to her, I mimic her pose and our elbows touch.

"How's the injuries?"

"Sore," I tell her honestly.

"I'll check them out tomorrow."

I grin. That means I'll get to see her again within twenty-four hours.

"Alright." I nod.

We stay side by side in silence, each of us drinking our beers as the music pumps outside and people gossip inside.

"What's blondie's deal? I'm getting the death stare."

I scan the room and I'm just about to ask her who she's talking about when a guy moves, and I see her.

Vanessa.

More affectionately known as the ex from hell.

"Christ, don't ask," I groan.

"She's really staring, champ, is she pissed off with me or you?" she asks, her tone amused.

"She's pissed off with *life*," I mutter.

"Disgruntled ex?" she questions, her elbow lightly bumping mine.

"Something like that," I mutter and run my hand through my hair.

She giggles again and I bump my shoulder into hers. "Don't laugh at me. That bitch is crazy."

"And that only makes it funnier." She grins.

Ramsey sits her bottle down on the bench top and I snag her arm, turning the bracelet on her wrist over in my fingers.

"What's this?"

She touches it, her fingers lightly brushing mine, and I try to ignore the tingle that runs down my spine.

"It's my charm bracelet. I collect little trinkets to remember things by."

I rest her wrist in one of my hands and put my drink down so I can use the other hand to look at the small gold charms.

"What's this one for?" I ask, holding a small palm tree between my fingers.

She grins. "Me and a few of the girls went on a tropical getaway a few years back, all we did was swim in the pool, drink cocktails and get hit on by the guys working at the resort." She smiles fondly at the memory. "It was the most relaxing week of my life."

The tone in her voice makes me smile.

"And this one?" I grasp a tiny charm that looks like a syringe.

She grimaces. "Juliet got me that, she's super allergic to bees and she got a sting one day – I had to stab her in the leg with her epi-pen."

"Let me guess, you're not big on needles?" I smirk.

"*Nope*. They tried to make me learn acupuncture for my physio degree, but I ended up getting an exemption due to all the fainting and throwing up."

I chuckle.

"Sorry." She frowns. "That was gross; I should really get a filter."

"Don't." I shake my head. "I like you unfiltered."

She gives me a shy smile.

"What's the story with this one?"

She leans in to see what I'm looking at and my nose fills with the scent of her. She smells like a bunch of flowers.

Pretty. She smells pretty. The same way she looks.

She giggles and glances up at me, her honey-coloured eyes sparkling. "That's a pushbike."

I raise my brows in question, waiting for the story.

She laughs. "It goes with the wine bottle." She points to a charm on the other side of the bracelet. "Have you ever done one of those pushbike pub crawls?"

"Can't say I have."

"You should." She grins. "I skinned my knees up so bad, but even still, what a freakin' day that was."

I turn the delicate bracelet around in my fingers. "Why do I get the feeling that you're kinda wild?"

She huffs out a laugh. "Maybe when I was seventeen. Now I get my kicks from muscles and joints."

"How old are you?"

She spins the bracelet around and points to a small '21' charm. "I'm nearly twenty-two."

"You're so young."

Too young for me.

She shrugs. "How old are you?"

"Twenty-seven, I'll be twenty-eight this year."

"Old man." She smirks.

My gaze travels across the room, and I find Vanessa boring holes into Ramsey, her evil stare focused entirely on the woman next to me.

"You're only as old as the woman you feel," I mumble.

She giggles, and I pull my eyes from the crazy chick across the room.

"Oh yeah? And what woman are you feeling, champ?"

You. I think to myself.

I would quite happily feel twenty-one again right now.

"No comment," I reply with a smirk.

"You could feel however old she is. I'm lucky looks can't kill." She tips her head in the direction of Vanessa, and I suddenly feel the need to get Ramsey away from here.

"You want to see upstairs?"

She turns, resting on one elbow, so she can look at me.

I do the same.

"This is your party, you don't have to spend all your time babysitting me."

"What if I want to?"

The words are out of my mouth before I can really consider the implications of them.

Her eyes sparkle. "Well then, lead the way."

CHAPTER SIX

Ramsey

"That's my room," he says, his voice gravelly as we pass an open bedroom door.

We're the only ones up here – apparently it goes without saying that you don't go where you're not welcome at Hudson's house.

My stomach flutters at the idea of being welcome here.

And with a personal tour guide, nonetheless.

"Oh, come see this, you'll love it." He grabs my hand and tows me along, and I let him.

I like the feel of my hand in his. His skin is warm and welcoming – a stark contrast to his hard, cool exterior.

He leads me into a big room with couches set up around a huge TV screen.

"Do you play?" He points at the gaming console on the table in front of the couch.

"Do *I* play?" I roll my eyes, sarcasm thick in my voice. "I don't just *play*, I kick ass."

He chuckles, deep and dark, and the butterflies in my belly stir again.

There's something so primal and edgy about this man. I should be running a mile – he's that terrifying, but I can't think of anything I want to do more than sit down on that couch next to him and play games.

He's more than just a hard, tough fighter who no one wants to fuck with – he's soft too, *tender*.

"Alright then, pinky, put your money where your mouth is."

I slide my hand from his and park myself on the couch, crossing my legs under me.

He reaches for the remote, hits the on button and turns on the gaming console.

The screen flickers to life, and he hands me a controller before sitting down right next to me.

He's so close that my knee is sitting half on top of his thigh. It's as hard as rock.

He runs a hand through the longer hair on the top of his head and I nibble on my bottom lip. He looks so sexy when he does that, and I don't think he has any idea.

"This okay?" he asks, his dark eyes searching my face.

I nod, even though I don't have a clue what game he's got in.

"I'll beat you at anything."

He chuckles. "We'll see."

The game intro comes on, and I laugh. It's an MMA fighter game.

"That's cheating."

He smirks at me in that devilish way that suits him so much. "Hey, you're the one who said you could beat me at *any-thing*."

"If I kick your ass in the cage, do I get to keep your title belts?"

His smirk deepens. "I think the UFC boss might have something to say about that."

"Pffft." I roll my eyes as I choose the biggest baddest-looking fighter the game has to offer. "Hey!" I giggle. "That one looks just like you."

He doesn't answer, and when I pull my eyes from the screen, I swear he's blushing.

"Oh my god, that *is* you, isn't it?" I demand.

"Maybe."

"You've been immortalised as a gaming character; do you know how jealous I am?"

A chuckle rumbles from deep in his chest. "Out of all my achievements, *that's* the thing you appreciate?"

I giggle. "Fake game blood I can handle," I explain.

"Of course," he muses as he selects his own character to fight against mine.

"I should warn you, I've got a killer spinning back kick."

Apparently his gaming character has the same strengths he does – a handful of his K.Os have been at the mercy of that kick.

"So I've heard," I drawl. "And you should know that I have one hell of a power punch," I inform him as I read the list of strengths my character has.

He chuckles.

We're in the virtual cage now, and while I can't watch a real fight, I'll have no problem watching animated characters punch and kick the shit out of each other.

"Show time, pinky." He smirks.

***

"I give up," I announce as I toss my controller onto the couch next to me.

He chuckles and leans back against the couch, his controller landing in his lap.

His grin is wide and easy – I get the feeling that I'm getting a rare glimpse into the man behind the mask.

"It's a shame you can't make money from gaming, then you wouldn't have to punch people for real," I say as I fall back against the plush cushions.

He kicked my ass. I only won one fight out of the eight or so we played. I don't know how long we've been hiding out up here, but I can still hear the pumping music coming from his back yard.

I sigh. "I should probably go find Juliet... let you get back to your friends."

I roll my head to the side and find he's watching me, his dark eyes probing.

"I like hanging out with you, Ramsey," he says quietly, *carefully* – his voice measured, almost as though he's not sure he should be saying the words. "I feel comfortable around you... like I've known you forever."

I try to swallow the lump in my throat.

I can't handle this, his intense stare, his words, his smell, the entire presence of the man is too much – too alluring, too tempting...

I know I can't go there – it would give Justin a heart attack.

I almost laugh at myself – the way I'm trying to convince myself that I can't have a man that probably has never even thought of me that way.

I'm his best friend's little sister – not some woman he has his eye on.

"I like hanging with you too," I admit. "It's easy. I feel like me when I'm with you."

His lips part and his tongue darts out to moisten them, and my entire body goes on high alert.

"Fuck it," I hear him mutter under his breath.

He leans in closer to me, his hand lightly brushing my thigh.

"What are you doing?" I whisper as he gets even closer, until our foreheads are touching.

"What I've wanted to do since the first moment I saw you," he replies, his voice a hoarse murmur.

My heart thumps in my chest.

He's about to kiss me. *Hudson Scott* is about to kiss *me*.

He leans in so our lips are only a fraction of an inch apart, I can feel his warm breath against mine.

I tip my face and our lips brush ever so softly.

He presses in again.

"Horror, you up here?" a voice calls loudly. My brother's voice.

"Shit," Hudson hisses.

I feel the whoosh of air as his face moves from mine, and I open my eyes.

I don't know what he sees when he looks at me, but he mouths the words 'I'm sorry'.

"In here, J," he calls loudly.

I suck in a deep breath.

Justin appears in the doorway, his eyes flickering between the two of us.

I don't know what the fuck I was thinking. I can't be up here kissing Hudson. I need a mental bitch slap to knock some sense into me.

We were *this* close to being caught by my brother.

I hope like hell I don't look as guilty as I feel, because if I do – we're screwed.

"Party for two?" Justin growls, his eyes narrowing at Hudson. He's suspicious.

Hudson chuckles lightly, like he hasn't got a care in the world. "We needed a break from the chaos. Vanessa was about ready to claw your sister's eyes out."

I hate the way he calls me 'your sister', it's as though he's giving himself a reminder that I'm forbidden territory.

"Who the fuck invited that bitch?" he asks with a frown.

"Rusty probably, you know he always likes to stir up trouble."

"*Rusty* is here?" I ask, my excitement genuine.

Justin nods. "Beast too. They just arrived… you better get down there, I left Juliet with them and they'll eat a sweet little thing like her alive." He frowns to himself as though he's only just realising his mistake.

I jump off the couch and hold my hand out to Hudson. "Rematch one day?"

He smirks and takes my hand in his. "Deal."

I stroll across the room towards the doorway. "You guys coming?"

Justin waves me off. "We'll be down in a minute."

I don't like the sound of that, but there's nothing I can do.

I need to put some serious distance between myself and the man I very nearly locked lips with.

I throw one last glance at Hudson before leaving the room hurriedly.

CHAPTER SEVEN

Hudson

I'm about to get the talk, and frankly, I deserve it.

I was about half a second away from claiming the lips of a woman I've been told to look out for – a woman who I've been warned off and instructed not to touch.

I'm a shitty human and an even worse mate, but *fuck*, I lose my head when it comes to Ramsey. I can't explain the pull I feel to her – it's like gravity.

Everything about her entices me – those long lashes around her golden eyes, her sexy body... even her damn pink hair.

I want to know more; I want to get closer. I *need* to.

But the look in Justin's eye right now informs me that I already know too much.

"Just say whatever's on your mind, J," I tell him as I set my controller on the coffee table next to Ramsey's and get up to hit the off button on the TV.

"Alright." He nods his head. "I don't like you being alone with my sister."

I cross my arms across my chest. "Why?"

"She's a chick, and they all seem to fall at your feet."

"And if she did... would that be so bad?"

He narrows his eyes at me. "You're asking if you sleeping with my sister would be a bad thing?"

I nod.

"You're lucky I don't knock your head in right here and now," he growls, crossing his own arms.

We're locked in a standoff now, and I don't know why the fuck I've pushed him on this – I knew before that she was off limits, but now he's spelling it out for me – leaving no room for doubt.

"I'm only going to say this once – Ramsey *isn't* yours to take. She doesn't fit in our lives; she's not some ringside hussy and she never will be. She's better than that."

I almost growl at him.

I'd never treat her like that. Not in a million years.

"I won't warn you again."

I hold my hands up in surrender. "We're just friends, J, I like her – she's not like the girls that hang around the fight scene."

"Friends." He tosses the word around like he's getting a feel for it. "As long as you don't fuck your friends, you and I won't have a problem.

I nod at him, one sharp bob of my head, and he returns the gesture.

We've just reached an understanding, one I'm not sure I can live with, but have to try to.

I'd rather have Ramsey as a friend than have nothing at all, and I don't know what I'd do if Justin wasn't in my life.

This is something I can't fuck with.

This is family.

"We better get back down there," he says, his arms relaxing from their tense position.

I follow him out of the room and down the stairs, and when I see Ramsey in Rusty's arms, being swung around in circles, my jaw ticks.

He sets her down on her feet and plants a kiss on her cheek.

"Maybe it's not me you need to be worried about," I say through clenched teeth.

***

"Hey, pinky."

She smiles shyly at me. "Come in."

I'm here for my physio appointment.

I might have seen her only last night, but it feels like an eternity.

It was the longest few hours of my life watching Rusty flirt with her in front of me – I've never wanted to hit a mate so badly. I guess that's how Justin felt about me.

I follow her into the room, and she closes the door behind me.

"How bad was the mess last night?" she asks as she gestures for me to climb onto the bed.

My leg has improved a little bit – all my niggles have actually, but not enough that I can even consider going back to training yet.

"I've had worse. Nothing a cleaner can't fix."

She goes to her desk and picks up her clipboard.

I don't know if she's really reading what's on there, or if she's just trying to avoid eye contact.

We haven't had a chance to talk about what happened between us last night and I'm dying to see if she's okay.

"Alright, let's start with your shirt off," she tells me, still not looking in my direction.

"Okay."

She sets down the clipboard and crosses the room to stand in front of me.

My legs drop open on auto pilot and she steps in between them. She reaches for the hem of my shirt and gently helps me take it off.

A shiver passes over my skin as her eyes graze over my body, still not making their way to my face.

She presses on a few tender spots and runs her hand down my neck and over my shoulder.

"Can we talk about what happened between us?" I ask in a whisper.

She freezes for a moment before starting her gentle massage of my neck again.

"What do you want to talk about?" she asks, her eyes flitting to mine for a fraction of a second before going back to her work.

God she's so fucking beautiful it hurts. She's not got a scrap of makeup on her face and her hair is piled messily on top of her head, but she's sexy as hell.

I want so badly to reach out and touch her again – find out what those lips feel like when they're really pressed against mine, but I can't do it.

No matter how much I want to.

"I kissed you."

"Barely," she breathes. There's a longing in her tone that makes my head hurt, because I feel the same way.

"I shouldn't have done that... we can't go there."

She digs her thumb in deeper, and I wince.

"Sorry," she says quickly. "Carry on."

She soothes the pain with her soft touch.

"Justin is my best mate, and I can't betray him like that."

"We got caught up... it's all good, just forget it happened."

I don't want to forget though – that's the god damn problem.

"Can we be friends? I wasn't joking when I said I like hanging out with you, Ramsey."

Her hands drop from my shoulders and she smiles at me. "I'd like that."

I dip my head, my grin growing.

"And I'm sorry that you had to listen to Justin give the big-brother speech – I bet that wasn't particularly enjoyable."

"He's just looking out for you. Keeping you safe from a meathead fighter."

"You're not a meathead, champ, you're just a teddy bear disguised as a killing machine."

That makes me laugh. "You reckon so?"

She nods, her nose scrunching up, a smile playing on the corner of her lip. "I know so."

CHAPTER EIGHT

Ramsey

"Have you got any more clients today?"

I shake my head and wipe my oily hands on a towel. "I don't actually work a Saturday – but you're the exception." I wink at him.

"Well now I feel like a douche," he says with a frown.

I laugh. "Don't. *Honestly*. It's not like I even had to go anywhere – you came to me. And speaking of, I'm sure you're used to people coming to you, so if you want to do this somewhere else, we can."

He shakes his head quickly. "I'm happy to come here."

"Alright... let me know if you change your mind."

"So, what are you up to now then?"

I shrug. "I might watch a movie. Juliet got called out to an emergency, so I don't know when she'll be back."

"Have you got popcorn?" he asks me.

I huff out a laugh. "I think there's a microwave pack in the kitchen... why?"

He grins wide. "I'm not staying if there's no popcorn."

I shake my head in amusement. "And who said I was inviting you to stay?"

He slides off the bench and reaches for his shirt. He shrugs it on gingerly, and I can't help but admire the fine specimen that he is.

The guy is so hot it's hard to look directly at him.

"We're friends now, pinky, friends watch movies."

I laugh. "Is that right?"

"So, what are we watching?" he asks as he walks to the door, his limp still visible.

I don't answer, and when he looks back at me over his shoulder, his hair falling in his eyes, my breath gets caught in my throat.

"Whatever you want," I choke out, and he grins again.

Jesus. Being this man's friend isn't going to be easy.

***

"You could have warned me that you were one of *those* people, you're lucky I've seen this movie at least a dozen times."

"You have?" He frowns at me. "Why didn't you say something?"

I shrug.

"And what do you mean 'one of *those* people'?"

I giggle. "One of those people that misses a plot point so asks what's going on and then is too busy talking and making incorrect guesses about what will happen next, that they miss the next plot point."

"I *don't* do that."

"You've done that for the past hour and a half – along with eating eighty percent of the popcorn."

He glances down at the bowl. "I didn't do that either." He grins.

"You're a liar, and not a very good one."

"Says the girl who keeps talking through the movie and eating all the snacks."

I bat his shoulder with the back of my hand and roll my eyes. "Shut up."

"Why don't you just save us both some time and tell me what happens," he suggests as he hits the mute button on the remote.

He's made himself right at home.

He's got his feet on the coffee table, and unlike when Justin does it, it doesn't bother me.

"They get together, and then she disappears. He's miserable, blah, blah, blah. They eventually get back together after a short airport terminal chase."

"Why is it always an airport chase with these chick movies?"

"That's romance for you, champ. And don't give me attitude about it, you picked the movie."

He grins, his dark eyes shining. "Don't tell anyone I watched that – I need people to be scared of me."

"People *are* scared of you," I reassure him as I rest my elbow on the back of the couch and my head in my hand.

"You think?"

"Do you not notice the wide berth people give you? Even your fans are wary of coming too close. You're one hell of a scary bastard, Hudson Scott."

"What about you? Do I scare *you*, Ramsey?"

He's looking at me with that intensity again, the one I feel right deep inside of me. The one that seems to make it impossible to lie, even when I know I should.

"You terrify me," I whisper.

I want to tell him that it's my heart that is scared, but the words get caught in my throat.

This is like déjà vu. He's got that gleam in his eye, the very same one as last night, right before he kissed me.

He must realise this moment is heading into territory he's just sworn away from because his head falls forward, a deep breath whooshing from his lungs.

When he looks back at me, there's a grin plastered across his face.

"I better get going."

I try to match his smile, but it doesn't really work.

I want to be friends with him, I really do... but it's hard when on the inside I want so much more than friendship.

I'm so into him, it's insane.

He pushes up from the couch and stretches his arms above his head.

I've had him shirtless, my hands on his bare skin more than once now, but the sight of that deep 'v' leading into the waist band of his shorts as his shirt rides up, is an entirely different sight.

"I'll see you on Tuesday?" I offer weakly.

"Tuesday." He nods in response.

I should get up and walk him to the door, but I need him out of my space so I can get my head on straight.

I'm all messed up over a guy – a fighter at that.

"See ya, pinky," he says as he crosses the room slowly.

"Later, champ."

I hear his feet moving down the hallway, the door opening and shutting and then he's gone.

And I already wish he'd come back.

CHAPTER NINE

Hudson

"You up for a run?" Justin asks.

"Fuck no. I'm still limping like an eighty-year-old. You know, for a head trainer, you're not very observant."

He chuckles. "Thought you might have just been milking it."

"Because that's my usual MO, right?"

He shrugs and goes back to scrolling on his cell phone. Facebook probably; the guy is addicted.

"What about him?" I tip my head in the direction of a ginger-haired kid sparring off to the side of the two rings we're meant to be scouting for talent.

"He's not even a senior."

"I know but check his footwork. He's young, but there's potential there."

Justin watches for a few moments before getting to his feet and heading in the direction of the kid.

I grin.

He might argue virtually *everything* with me, but he knows I've got an eye for talent.

I try to pick out a few fighters a year from the wrong side of the tracks and give them an all-expenses-paid membership at the MMA gym I fight from – Justin's dad's gym.

I might have grown up on the good side of town, but I know what it's like to struggle. My parents don't support my career – never have. So, when I left school at seventeen with the goal to pursue a career in fighting, I was cut off.

The only person I still speak to in my family is my older brother, and even that relationship is strained. If he wasn't my accountant, I'd probably never hear from him either.

Where I grew up, using your fists to make money isn't an acceptable career choice – it never mattered how good I was at it.

Justin, Rusty, Beast and the other guys at the gym – they're my real family.

People say blood is thicker than water, but I think that's bullshit. You're born with blood, but water is a choice.

"He gone fishing for newbies?"

I glance up and see Rusty standing in front of me.

He tips his head in the direction of Justin, who is now talking to the ginger-haired kid.

"Kid had good feet," I explain.

He nods and drops into the seat next to me.

We both watch as Justin speaks and the young guy's eyes light up.

"Got him," Rusty murmurs as Justin hands over a business card and then points in my direction.

The kid's jaw falls open, and I raise my chin at him, a chuckle falling from my lips.

"Kid's star struck," Rusty drawls.

"What are you doing here anyway?"

"Beast said you guys were down here, and I was bored."

I shake my head at him. "You've got a fight in less than a month, go and fucking train for it."

Out of all of us, Rusty is by far the least motivated. He's also the most naturally talented, so the fucker usually manages to get by on that.

He chuckles. "Yeah, maybe later... I was thinking of swinging by to see Ramsey."

My jaw clenches, but I chant to myself to stay cool.

I've got no reason and no right to get wound up at the idea of Ramsey and Rusty hanging out, but I can't seem to get that message to my racing pulse.

"Oh yeah? You nursing an injury?"

"Nope. Just wanted to hang out."

I nod my head, one sharp, short bob, my eyes trained on the two fighters in the ring throwing jabs at one another.

"I haven't seen her for a year or so, but *damn*, the girl is all grown up," he carries on, seemingly oblivious to my inner rage.

"I wouldn't let J hear you say that."

He chuckles. "What? That his sister is hot as fuck?"

I clench my fists and inhale deeply through my nose.

His chuckle deepens. "Shit, Horror, I thought Beast was making shit up, but he's right, isn't he? You're keen on Ramsey?"

My head snaps around to glare at him.

He howls with laughter at the look on my face.

"Shit, son, you're screwed."

"I don't know what the fuck you're talking about."

"Your knuckles are so white I'm worried you're going to pop a joint."

I glance down at my still tightly clenched fists and release them quickly.

Shit.

"We're friends. That's it. She's working on my injuries," I hiss.

"Is that what the kids are calling it these days?"

"Fuck off, Rusty."

"Don't bullshit me, Horror, you might be able to talk smack to Justin, but I'm smarter than him, and I know a lie when I see one."

"I'm almost entirely certain you're *not* smarter than him."

"Well I am. And seeing as you're thinking about banging your best mate's sister, I must be smarter than you too."

"I'm *not* thinking about fucking Ramsey."

He claps me on the shoulder and bounces to his feet.

"Well then you must be the only one," he taunts me.

I lunge for him, but he darts out of the way – stupid bastard and his uninjured body.

He chuckles, his loud laugh ringing out through the run-down old gym as he strolls out the door.

Justin looks at me in question, and I wave him off as I limp back to my seat.

Fucking Rusty and his bullshit.

He's so much easier to deal with when he's not right.

***

"What's Ramsey's cell number?" I ask Justin as he drops me back at my car.

I feel like a tool driving that car most of the time, but it's fast, and it used up some of the money I earnt from my fights. I earn more than I can figure out how to spend without living like a total wanker, so a ridiculously expensive car seemed like an acceptable purchase.

"What the fuck do you want that for?" he demands.

"Dude. *Chill.* She's my fucking physiotherapist, remember? I'm running late for our appointment, so I need to call her."

He grimaces. "Sorry, man, it's fucking Rusty – he's been in my ear all morning about Ramsey and I'm on edge."

I nod and feel like a total asshole. I'm the one testing the boundaries, not Rusty – well not as far as I'm aware.

"I'll keep an eye on him."

He grabs his phone and scrolls through.

"Thanks, bro." He calls out her number and I tap the digits into my contact list.

"I gotta boost, J, I'll talk to you tomorrow."

"Say hey to Ram-Ram for me," he calls as I slam the door shut.

I try to jog over to my car, but my leg is still giving me grief.

I hate being injured. My body runs like a well-oiled machine usually, and the week or so after a tough fight drives me insane.

I start my engine and it purrs to life. I turn out of the gym car park and head down the street towards Ramsey's, hitting dial on the Bluetooth car system.

Her phone rings and rings, and I'm just about to hang up when her breathy voice answers, "Hello?"

Just the sound of her speaking ties me up in knots.

"Hello?" she repeats.

"Ramsey, hey, it's Hudson."

"Oh hey, champ." I can hear the smile in her voice.

I can't pinpoint the moment she started calling me champ, but I like it.

"I got caught up at the gym, I'm really sorry, I'm still ten away... do you want to rebook me?"

"It's no worries, you're my last client for the day, so take your time."

"You're too good to me."

"Special privileges remember?" She laughs lightly.

"I'll see you soon."

"Drive safe," she replies, her tone soft.

I hit the end key and try to steady my thumping heart.

There is just something about Ramsey Ashton that turns me into a complete wreck.

CHAPTER TEN

Ramsey

He winces as he throws his legs over the side of the bed.

I got stuck into his sore spots today – I know he can handle it, and he needs to get back to training, so the sooner we get that muscle in working order again, the better.

"What are you up to tonight?" I ask as he slides his shirt on.

I've learnt to look away when he does that – it's better for my self-control.

"No big plans. Might play some video games."

"Rager of a night," I joke.

He chuckles. "What about you then? What big, exciting plans have you got?"

"Grocery shopping." I screw up my nose as I turn around. Thankfully, he's fully clothed now.

His chuckle deepens. "And you're giving *me* shit?"

I pop a shoulder and grin. "I'm starving and there is no food in this house. Juliet has been a total piker and gone to her mum's house for dinner."

He's silent for a few beats.

"Come out for dinner with me then."

It's not a question.

"Dinner? With *you*?" I nibble on my bottom lip nervously.

I know we've agreed to be friends, and friends go out for dinner, but that sounds a lot like a date.

"Yeah," he says, his dark eyes burning into mine.

He doesn't elaborate further. He doesn't reassure me that it's not a date... he just stares and waits for me to say yes; because I think we both already know that I will.

I watch him, watching me, my resolve weakening by the second.

"So... where are you taking me?"

***

"You like sushi, right?"

"There are people out there who *don't* like sushi?"

He smirks. "There's some sick individuals in the world, pinky, I don't know what to tell you."

A wide, genuine smile graces my face. I like hanging out with this man far too much.

I can already feel that this is going to end in heartbreak, for me at least.

"This is the best sushi in town."

I should know that. This is *my* home town after all, but since I haven't spent any time here in the past few years, it's all different now than it was when I left.

So much has changed around here.

The installation of a world-class fighting gym being one of the main things – courtesy of my dad.

There were never this many sexy fighters wandering around when I was in high school. I probably would have got myself into a whole heap of trouble if there was.

He holds the glass door open for me and points in the direction of a vacant booth down the back.

Heads turn as we walk past, but Hudson doesn't seem to notice. No one approaches us. In fact, no one even gets out their phone to take a photo.

Either the novelty of living in the same town as a superstar athlete has worn off – which I doubt due to the amount of whispering going on – or Hudson really does scare people.

I guess they don't call him 'Horror' for nothing.

He slides into one side of the booth and I take the other – so we're sitting directly opposite one another.

His face has healed up quickly – the black eye is just a faint yellow bruise now, and his jaw has only got a little bit of purple left.

He pushes a menu in my direction. "You've never been here?"

"Nope."

"How long have you been away for?"

"Long enough for the MMA boys to take over the town," I reply with a grin.

He chuckles. "Yeah, sorry about that."

I shrug. "Hey, it should be good for business at least. I need a heap of beat-up bodies to fix. And it's not your doing – it's my father's."

He smirks and glances down at his menu.

"How long have you lived here?" I ask, paying no attention whatsoever to what I'm going to eat.

I'm still starving, but just as much for information about him as I am for food.

"About four, maybe four and a half years now. I met Justin when I'd been here about six months and we've been close ever since."

"Where's your family from?"

He drops his menu and studies me. "A stuck-up town about three hours from here. They all still live there, my mum, dad, and my brother. We're not exactly close."

"That sucks."

I might not be super close with my parents either, but I have my brother at least.

He shrugs. "It is what it is. I've got plenty of people in my corner."

I smile. "I'm in your corner, hypothetically speaking at least."

He grins widely, showing off his perfectly-straight white teeth. "You don't want to hang out on the side of the cage again?"

I shudder. "I'll pass. Why do they have to call it a cage anyway? It makes you sound like an animal."

"You should open your eyes next time I fight, pinky... I *am* an animal."

A shiver crawls over my skin, leaving goose bumps in its wake.

He really is a scary guy.

The waitress appears then to take our drink order and when she leaves, the dark intensity burning in his eyes has lightened.

"You went to school here?"

I nod. "Left to study physio after I graduated high school."

"Is that how you know Juliet?"

"Yeah, we've been friends since I was about eight. She started her vet nurse degree at another school but transferred to be closer to me in her second year, my first year – she's a year older than me."

"Cute."

"That word sounds weird coming out of your mouth."

He chuckles. "Why?"

"Rugged men that look like they could rip you in half don't usually say words like 'cute'..."

"Pretty girls with pink hair don't usually talk about a big bad, MMA fighter *'ripping them in half'*." He grins deviously, the sexual innuendo dripping from his lips.

"Oh my god, I didn't say it like *that*." I feel my cheeks heat. "I meant with your bare hands."

"Just stop talking, pinky, you're already pretty deep in that hole."

Oh sweet Jesus.

"Now who's saying inappropriate shit, huh?" I giggle.

He laughs, long and loud. "You know, Ramsey, I haven't laughed like this in a long time."

"Whatever. You're *always* laughing and smiling."

He shakes his head. "It's only when I'm with you."

I blush.

"Seriously, ask anyone, a scowl is my usual expression. You're going to be bad for my rep if this carries on – people will start asking me for photos and to sign shit if I'm not careful."

"They don't ever ask you?" I question, grateful for the slight shift in conversation. I didn't quite know what to say when he was being so sweet.

He shrugs. "Nah, not many are brave enough... I pride my-self on being unapproachable."

Sure, he might look as hard as nails, but he's never made me feel anything *but* welcome.

I glance behind me and see a young guy at a nearby table raising his phone to take a photo of Hudson, doing his best to be inconspicuous. I duck out of the way.

I've had enough of that shit with my dad to last me a life-time.

Unlike Hudson, my dad prized himself on being approach-able, and my childhood suffered because of it.

We had to stop and talk to *every* fan – *every* fighter. We'd go on family holidays that consisted of nothing much more than visiting the local gyms and recruiting fighters.

While I agree that there's something noble in the way my father made time for everyone, it would have been nice if just once he made time for me.

Justin loved it, obviously – it was an aspiring fighter's wet dream to have a father like ours.

"You're not close to your folks?" I ask him.

He shakes his head. "They don't approve of my career choice."

I clasp my chest in mock outrage. "What mother doesn't like to see her baby getting beaten half to death at the hands of another man?"

He chuckles. "If I'm doing it right, I'm the one who's doing the beating."

He is doing it right. I know that much.

"I didn't expect them to be there in the front row of every fight, but I thought they'd support me, not disown me."

There's hurt there in his eyes that I'd be willing to bet he rarely shows.

"You don't talk to them at all?"

"My mum sends a card on Christmas and my birthday."

I reach out across the table and take his hand in mine without thinking twice about it.

"That's really shitty, champ."

He shrugs, his fingers weaving through mine. "That's life for you."

"What about your brother? You see much of him?"

"A little bit," he replies, his gaze locked on our intertwined hands. "He's my accountant. I think he's a little more understanding since he sees the balance of my bank account – not that I do it for the money."

"I bet the money doesn't hurt though."

He grins, his face tipping up to look at me. "It certainly doesn't."

The waitress comes back with our drinks, and I reluctantly pull my hand from his.

She takes our food order and disappears again.

"So, what about you? Close with your olds?"

I shake my head as I take a sip of my chocolate milkshake. "Not really. If you're not a fighter, you don't really exist in my father's eyes. And if you don't exist in his eyes, then my mother doesn't really see you either."

He frowns. "That's fucked up."

"That's life for you," I repeat his words back to him. "It's not like they were horrible to me or anything like that. I had everything I needed. They bought me a car when I turned sixteen, they paid for college... I dunno – I guess I just missed out on anything genuine from them."

"I see him around a lot – your dad."

"I bet he loves you," I say with a roll of my eyes.

He winks at me. "He's so far up my ass it's almost embarrassing."

Laughter bubbles out of me. "Oh my god, I can't believe you just said that."

He chuckles. "It's true. He's like that with all the pro guys who train there."

"He was heartbroken when Justin got that injury and couldn't fight anymore. He had plans for him to be a big-time champion. Maybe he's living through you to fill that void his disappointing children left."

The smile slides off his lips and he looks at me hard. "You could *never* be a disappointment, Ramsey – not even if you tried."

A nervous giggle escapes my lips as I try to brush away his comment, but he isn't having it.

"You're smart, funny and beautiful. Don't let your dad acting like a dick *ever* make you believe otherwise."

"Okay," I whisper.

He raises his brows at me.

"Okay," I say with more volume.

"Okay," he repeats.

CHAPTER ELEVEN

Hudson

"My sister fixed you up yet or what?" Justin demands as I stroll into the gym.

"Almost as good as new." I nod.

I already *am* as good as new if I'm being honest, but I may or may not be holding onto these injuries with everything I've got so I can justify visiting her house every couple of days like I have been the past few weeks.

She schedules me in at the end of her work day and then we hang out afterwards.

Sometimes Juliet is with us, Justin too on the odd occasion, but more often than not, we're alone, and it's the highlight of my week.

We even went to the gym for a workout together earlier in the week so she could check on my form and run me through a few stretches.

I realised the minute I got there that I'd made a grave mistake. She works out in the tiniest pair of shorts and a crop top. Her whole body was right there for me to ogle and ogle it I did. Especially that sexy damn ass of hers that looked too good in those shorts.

"You ready to get back into some light sparring?" Justin asks, excitement shining in his eyes.

"Give it a few more days until Ramsey gives me the all clear."

"She's babying you," he grumbles. "You look fine to me."

"She's the one with the degree." I cross my arms across my chest and shoot him a smug look.

He mutters something else under his breath.

"You're doing some weight training then, you look weak."

"Fuck off," I shoot back. "I could still kick your ass and you know it."

He grins. "Put your money where your mouth is then, big shot."

"I'm not stupid, I know when I'm being baited, shithead."

He chuckles. "You've been spending too much time with Ramsey; you're starting to sound like her."

That gets a laugh out of me.

Justin has chilled out about me and Ramsey hanging out. It's been about a month since we met now, and nothing has happened between us – not since that night at my house.

I figure he thinks he's in the clear.

He obviously hasn't taken a look inside my mind lately. I'd be a dead man if he had.

I'm *craving* her.

Every minute I spend in her company only intensifies the feelings growing inside my chest.

Every time she laughs, I find myself smiling wider.

It's as though every action of hers has a direct reaction inside of me.

I'm becoming obsessed with Ramsey Ashton and there's not a damn thing I can do to stop it.

"You're coming to watch Rusty tomorrow night, right?"

"For the hundredth time, yeah, I'll be there."

Justin has been helping out with Rusty's prep for the past few weeks while I've been out of action.

It's not a top-class fight, but it's his toughest fight to date.

Hell, I think even he's realised that and started to put his head down and get some work done these past few weeks.

"He gonna make weight?" I question as I glance across the room to where Rusty is skipping, about four layers of clothing on his body.

"He fucking better. I caught the bastard eating chicken nuggets last week. He was a kilo over this morning, so the fucker has been skipping for the past half hour."

"He'll sweat it out."

"I'll kill him myself if he doesn't make that fight."

"You're awfully filled with rage today, what's up your ass?"

He scowls at me. "*Nothing.*"

"Girl problems?" I ask, the corner of my mouth twitching.

"Nope," he grinds out.

Definitely girl problems.

"Well I'm headed for the weights. Let me know if you decide it's female related after all."

I get about three steps away when he cracks.

"So, there's this chick, right?"

I turn back around. "Alright."

"We've kinda had a thing going for a while now."

We both know he's talking about Juliet.

I don't know who he thinks he's fooling, but I'll humour him.

"I dunno, man." He runs his hand through his dark blond hair. "Maybe she finally got sick of my shit... she's going on a date tonight with some dude she met at work."

"Ouch."

"What the fuck am I meant to do about it?"

"I assume you've considered manning the hell up and telling her how you feel?"

He scowls at me. "You make it sound like it's as simple as that."

I shrug at him. "The only one making it hard is *you*."

"Fuck off."

I shake my head at him. "I've got shit to do today, bro, can't stand here all day giving you advice that you're going to ignore. You either let her go and enjoy her date, or you find your balls and go get her before it's too late. Your call."

I carry on heading for the weights equipment.

This is a fucking gym not a therapy office, for fuck's sake.

I need to get back into some gloves, no one bothers me with this kind of shit when I'm throwing punches.

"Horror," Justin calls.

I huff out a breath. He better be done with this deep and meaningful shit.

"I've got your ticket for tomorrow."

I tip my chin to him in thanks from where I am.

"You're seeing Ramsey again tomorrow, right?"

I nod.

"I've got tickets for her and Juliet too, can you take them?"

I shake my head in amusement. "Why the hell is she coming to another fight?"

"Rusty made her feel guilty." He grins.

"You guys are assholes," I reply as I slip my earbuds into my ears and hit play on my workout playlist.

The heavy beat takes over and blocks out everything. Well, *almost* everything.

***

"I don't know why I do this to myself." Ramsey sighs as she slips on her jacket.

Juliet giggles. "Just think of all the abs."

Ramsey's eyes dart to mine and she laughs. "I told you she only wanted to come to perve."

Juliet blushes.

"How was your date last night?" I ask her casually.

"It was okay..." She frowns at me. "How did *you* know I had a date?"

"Word on the street." I smirk.

Ramsey eyes me curiously.

"You gonna see him again?" I question.

She fiddles with a loose thread on the bottom of her skirt. "I'm not sure... I guess I'll just see how it goes."

"Holding out for something better, Jules?" I ask with a wink.

She blushes a deep scarlet and virtually leaps to her feet. "I forgot to put something in my bag," she says as she rushes from the room.

"What the hell was that all about?" Ramsey demands.

I glance at her over the back of the couch and shake my head in amusement at the look on her face. "Nothing you need to worry about."

"Do you know how long it took me to convince her to go on that damn date? And here you are, encouraging her to ditch the guy. What the fuck, champ?"

"You're a smart girl, pinky, I bet you can figure it out." I smirk.

She narrows her eyes at me and points her finger at my chest. "If you even so much as utter my brother's name, I'm going to skin you alive."

"Would it be so bad, your brother and your best friend?"

"It would be wrong on *so* many levels; he's always looked out for her like a brother – since she was about ten years old. It would be like kissing a sibling." She shudders.

I chuckle. "Well maybe they don't see it that way."

She takes a step towards me, her finger jabbing into my collarbone. "Wash your mouth out."

I wrap my hand around hers and tug. She stumbles forward, and I grab her hip, dragging her over the back of the couch and half into my lap.

She shrieks with laughter, shoving at me as she lands.

She's so close I can smell her perfume.

She wiggles against my hold and grins up at me. "Brute."

I can't get over that smile on her face – especially when it's directed at me.

She's like nobody else in my life.

She sees past the tough exterior to the man inside, and when she looks at me like that, it's easy to believe she likes what she sees.

I reach out and twist a strand of pink hair between my fingers.

Her lids close momentarily before fluttering open again, her golden eyes burning into mine.

I could lean in and kiss her right now, consequences be damned. I know she feels this between us, I can see it in her eyes – hear it in her voice when she talks to me.

She wants me as badly as I want her.

I lean in.

"Alright, let's go!" Juliet yells from down the hall, snapping us both out of the moment.

Ramsey scrambles from my lap to her feet, smoothing down her jeans and top as she goes. I copy, standing a foot away from her.

Juliet strolls through the room towards the front door, totally oblivious to the sexual tension in the air.

"You two coming or what?" she yells when we don't follow.

"Just grabbing my bag," Ramsey yells back, but she doesn't move an inch.

She just stands there, staring back at me.

We're both still on our own side of the invisible line we've drawn in the middle of our relationship, but we're so close to the edge.

I for one, am pressed so close up to that line I'm almost standing on it, and she's right there with me, toe to toe.

I know she's doing the same thing I am – weighing up in her head about whether or not we can do this... how we can possibly be together when we both know what it would do to Justin.

"We should go," Ramsey whispers.

"We should," I agree.

"Hudson," she breathes as I take a step closer – effectively crossing the line.

"Ramsey," I murmur.

"That's it, I'm driving myself!" Juliet yells from out front.

Ramsey huffs out a laugh and smiles sweetly up at me. "Let's go, champ."

She steps around me and walks to the door, and I release a deep breath.

I just came so close to fucking everything up and I honestly don't even know if I care enough to make sure it doesn't happen again.

CHAPTER TWELVE

Ramsey

"I'm just going to go check in with Rusty," Hudson tells us once he's escorted us to our seats – front freakin' row – again.

I already feel nauseous and there's not even any fighters out here yet.

Fucking Rusty and his guilt trip.

He better not bleed tonight or I think I might actually puke.

"Ramsey?" his voice comes again.

I pull my eyes from the cage and raise my brows at him. "Sorry, *what*?"

He searches my face. "I said I'm just going to shoot out back, you girls alright here?"

"We're good thanks. Tell him if he starts bleeding, I'm leaving."

He grins wickedly. "I'll be sure to pass that on."

Juliet sits down, but I stay standing, unable to pull my eyes from the sexiest man in the world as he stalks across the room, once again turning heads as he goes.

"You think you'll be able to see past those love hearts in your eyes?"

"Probably not." I sigh as he disappears from sight.

"Did he finally kiss you on the couch or what?"

My jaw drops as I sit down in the seat next to her.

"You saw us?"

"Hell *yes,* I saw you… that chemistry is *off* the charts. Why do you think I shot through the room like a cat on a hot tin roof? I thought the two of you might have finally been going to get on with it."

I sigh. "Nope. So close yet so far."

"You should try making him jealous."

I pop a brow. "What, like you're trying to do with Justin?"

Her eyes widen and her cheeks change colour.

"I don't know what you're talking about."

"Sure you don't," I mutter under my breath. "And besides, I don't want to make him jealous. We're friends – I don't want to hurt him."

She snorts out a laugh. "Oh *please.* You two are never going to be 'just friends', that ship sailed the moment you saw each other, and you know it."

"But Justin—"

"But Justin *nothing*," she interrupts, "he's a big boy – he'll get over it. I'm sure he just wants you to be happy when it comes down to it."

I'm pretty sure he wants me to be celibate, but whatever.

"What makes you think that Hudson would make me happy?"

She sighs wistfully at something over my shoulder. "*Look* at him… do you think there's ever been a woman enter his bed and leave anything other than happy?"

"Ew." I scrunch up my nose and scowl at her as I think about other women in his bed. "That was a visual I didn't need."

"Even his walk is sexy."

I turn and glance at him over my shoulder and my breath gets caught in my throat when he offers me a sexy, devious grin.

"Girl, when he looks at you like that, even *I* get turned on."

I burst into laughter so hard it hurts my ribs.

"What's so funny?" Hudson asks as he slides into the chair next to me, an amused expression on his face as he hands me and Juliet a beer each.

I wipe at the tears in my eyes before taking the bottle from him. "Thanks, and don't worry – private joke."

He takes a pull of his own beer, his dark eyes never leaving mine.

He doesn't question me again, but it feels like he's somehow getting the answers he wants anyway.

"Is he ready?" I question.

"As ready as Rusty ever is." He shakes his head in disapproval.

"Did you warn him to keep his blood inside his body?"

He smirks. "I did. He said to tell you that you might want to close your eyes."

"Well that fills me with confidence," I mutter as I take a big gulp of my drink.

Maybe if I get drunk, I won't be so bothered.

"Where's the hotties? I'm ready for the show." Juliet bounces in her seat excitedly.

"Right here, babe." I hear my brother's voice behind us.

I don't miss the way Juliet's eyes light up, or the way Justin appraises her body, head to toe, before sitting down next to her.

Fuck it all. Hudson was right. This isn't just friendly banter.

My best friend is in love with my brother. My brother has a thing for my friend. For fuck's sake.

I turn and glare at Hudson, as though this is somehow his doing.

He raises his brows at me and holds up his hands in surrender. "Don't shoot the messenger, pinky."

I'm about to start my grumbling when the lights die down and the music starts.

A spotlight appears in the middle of the cage and I squeeze my eyes shut in anticipation.

"Relax, Ramsey, they haven't even come out yet." His voice is right at my ear, warm and smooth.

I pry open one eye. He's right. There's no one here to bleed. Yet.

I blow out a deep breath.

Hudson chuckles and leans back in his chair, his long arm coming around the back of my seat.

I feel him playing with my hair and butterflies erupt in my stomach.

I can't take much more of this silent dance that's going on between us.

We're weaving in and out of reach of one another. Getting just close enough to touch and then darting out of the way.

It's exhausting.

It's exhilarating.

It's not enough.

His thumb brushes my bare arm and my skin is set alight.

Jesus. It's not even *close* to being enough.

I hear the announcer speaking – introducing Rusty's opponent, and the blaring music of his walkout song fills the room.

He's got a lot of support here tonight.

The stadium fills with cheers and whoops.

"Here he comes," Justin says, his knee jiggling up and down nervously.

As glad as I am that he's not in that cage anymore, it makes me sad to know he's been forced to give up competing in a sport he loves.

"And in the blue trunks with the gold trim, we have Rusty 'Rager' Gordon," the voice booms out over the sea of people.

Hudson flies to his feet, tugging me with him as a loud, pulsing beat fills the air.

I clap my hands together, nerves flitting through my body as Rusty jogs right past us, Hudson clapping him on the shoulder as he goes.

Beast is there with him and a couple of other guys I don't recognise – trainers from the gym most likely.

"Let's go, Rusty, you've got this!" Justin yells as Rusty starts jogging around the cage, the crowd going crazy.

He shrugs off his blue and gold robe, and Beast takes it from him.

His body is ripped to shreds, and I'm glad that Juliet is getting the view she was hoping for – at least one of us might enjoy this event.

"You good?" Hudson asks, his arm finding its spot around me again as we sit down.

"Not really," I admit.

He chuckles.

"Tell me if you think you're going to puke."

"No deal."

There's no way I'm spewing in front of him. And besides, I'm more likely to faint than I am to blow chunks, but passing out again would be more than embarrassing enough.

I just have to remember to keep my head down when they start throwing punches.

My stomach lurches at the idea of it.

Damn Rusty. He owes me big time for this.

The two men dance around the cage, working combos and playing up for the crowd.

I can feel my pulse racing and I decide that I'm going to pick a spot on the floor to look at right now before they get this thing started.

I find the remnants of an old piece of chewing gum squished and dried on the ground just in front of my feet and I stare at it as though my life depends on it.

"Here they go," Hudson murmurs in my ear, his hold around my shoulders tightening slightly.

As much as I hate coming to these things, I'd probably do it all again if it meant I got to feel safe and protected in his arms like this.

The crowd starts going wild as the fight gets underway and I hear the unmistakable sound of punches and kicks being thrown.

Justin is screaming something about a right uppercut, but I can't look.

Hudson yells for Rusty to take it to the floor, and I hear a loud thud that sounds suspiciously like two bodies hitting the mats.

Juliet gasps and squeaks the word, "*No*," and I don't know what the hell I'm thinking, but I look up.

Rusty has his opponent pinned to the ground, and there is blood *everywhere*. I don't even know whose blood it all is, but I know it's more than I can handle.

My mouth starts to salivate and yellow splotches appear in my vision.

"Shit," I hear Hudson say before everything goes black.

CHAPTER THIRTEEN

Hudson

"C'mon, pinky, wake up, beautiful."

I blow gently in her pale face.

She's as white as a ghost.

This is the second time I've seen her drop like this, and I can't help but think of the irony of it all; she's got one foot in the world of fighting, yet she can't stomach a single thing about it.

She makes a small moaning noise, but her eyes don't open.

I glance around the empty foyer where I've carried her and assess my options.

I could take her to the team doctor, and have him look her over, but judging by that knee to the ribs that Rusty took out there, I'd say he's going to have his hands full already.

I'm sure she'll be fine when she wakes up, I'd just prefer that she got the fuck on with it already.

Juliet bursts through the door, a giant smile on her face. "He won!"

"Tin-ass bastard." I grin.

"It was *so* gross." She shudders.

I chuckle. She doesn't look like it was too much of an effort for her to be a part of.

"Where's Justin?"

"Rusty wanted him out back for something so I thought I'd come check on sleeping beauty."

"She's still out."

"She's probably faking it – she's going to die of embarrassment."

I glance back down at the woman in my arms. Some of the colour is returning to her cheeks.

I gently run my finger down the side of her face.

"You really care for her, don't you?"

My eyes flash to Juliet in surprise, denial quick on my lips. "She's Justin's sister, he'd kill me if I didn't look out for her."

Juliet snorts out a laugh. "Is that how this is going to go? You're going to sit there and pretend this is about doing a favour for your mate? *Please*."

I scowl at her.

"You don't fool me, you might look like a big tough guy, but you're soft as a marshmallow when it comes to that girl and you know it."

She's one hundred percent fucking right. I'm just not willing to admit it.

Not to anyone other than myself anyway.

She sighs when I don't answer.

"What are you going to do with her when she wakes up?"

"I'll take her home."

"I can drive you," she offers.

I shake my head, my gaze falling back to Ramsey. "Nah that's okay, you stay and watch the rest of the card with Justin, I'll walk her home – the fresh air might do her good." I tip my head in the direction of the front door.

It's not too long of a walk – might feel that way if I have to carry her though.

She eyes me knowingly. "Alright then, hot shot." She tosses me Ramsey's jersey and turns to go back through the doors and into the main arena but pauses and looks back at us. "I'm just going to say this once..."

I nod for her to go on.

"Please don't break her heart. I know she acts tough, but deep down, she's not – so just don't hurt her, okay?"

I don't know how I could possibly break something I don't have, but I find myself nodding my head regardless, the warning I didn't know I required has been heeded.

"And thanks, Hudson, for taking care of her... I know she's safe with you – physically at least."

She's safe with me alright – injured or not, I'd kill anyone that tried to hurt her – rip them limb from limb.

I nod at Juliet once and she disappears back through the door.

I let out a deep breath and run my hand through my hair.

I don't know what the hell I'm doing.

I'm getting in deep – too deep with this girl and I'm not sure I'll be able to get back out.

I huff out another breath and look down to the woman who is slowly but surely, stealing my heart.

Her wide golden eyes are looking back at me.

"Finally," I whisper. "I was starting to get worried."

"What happened?" she breathes as she tries to sit up.

I press down on her shoulder and hold her in place. "Take it easy, you fainted."

She groans and brings a hand up to cover her face. "Not *again*."

"I'm afraid so, but in your defence, there was a *lot* of blood."

She grimaces.

"Sorry. Too soon."

She takes a deep breath and relaxes in my arms.

"Did you have to carry me out?"

I nod.

She groans again and turns her head so her face is hidden in my t-shirt. "You could have made Justin do it."

"He tried. I wouldn't let him."

She peeks out at me. "Why not?"

Why not? What a loaded question that is.

Because I wanted to hold you.

Because the idea of you being away from me makes me feel anxious.

Because I want to take care of you.

Because you're mine.

"I didn't want him to miss the fight," I say instead, the lie rolling off my tongue like the truth.

"Oh shit, I made you miss Rusty's fight?" She tries to scramble from my lap, but I'm stronger than her, and she's not going anywhere – especially not for a fight I couldn't care less about.

"*Relax*. The fight is over – Rusty won."

"He did?" she asks, her voice rising an octave in excitement.

I nod.

"Oh yay!"

I chuckle. She's too fucking sweet. She hates the sport, but she still attends. She faints at the sight of blood, but she's still thrilled that her friend won.

Ramsey Ashton is too good.

Certainly too good for a guy like me.

"Justin and Juliet are going to stay and watch the rest of the fights."

She rolls her eyes, and I laugh.

"But you and me, pinky, we're headed home."

She shakes her head quickly. "You can go back in and watch, I've already hijacked enough of your night."

I pin her with my stare. "If you think I'm going to do anything other than walk you home, then you don't know me very well."

"Okay," she breathes, blinking slowly.

"You think you can stand?" I ask as I gingerly ease her up so she's sitting in my lap.

She blushes as her hand brushes my crotch.

"I'm fine. I'm really sorry about this."

She might be sorry, but I'm not. I'd hold her like this all day if I could.

I stand, with my arms still holding her against me.

Her eyes never leave mine as her feet find the floor.

She's clinging onto my shoulders and our bodies are flush together.

If Justin were to walk out and see this, he'd kick my ass.

"Thank you for taking care of me," she whispers before her tongue darts out and moistens her lips.

She's so sexy, even when she's not trying to be.

I'm just about to let her go when she leans in closer, her lips brushing my cheek.

Justin would *definitely* kick my ass for that.

Hell, I'd be dead if he knew what I was thinking about when it came to the woman in front of me.

She glances at my jacket and her jersey. "You ready to go home?" she asks, and I allow myself for just a moment to believe that it's an invitation.

***

I look down at our joined hands swinging between us and feel like a teenager out with a girl for the first time.

I'm anything but an innocent teenager anymore, one look in the mirror gets that message across loud and clear, but shit, this woman makes me feel like one anyway.

I managed to hold her hand under the pretence of her feeling faint, but I think we both know that was a lie.

She's fine. I was right, the fresh air was the best thing for her.

We've got a twenty-minute walk ahead of us. I wish it was five times as long, because I know once I walk her to her door, there's going to be nothing left to do except get in my car and drive myself back to my big, empty house.

That's not what I want.

She's what I want.

"How'd you get into fighting?" she asks, her eyes shining in the moonlight.

"I did Taekwondo as a kid, then Jiu Jitsu and Karate, I've got more black belts than I know what to do with, but I was never quite satisfied. I tried boxing, kickboxing and then I found my way into an MMA gym." I shrug. "I guess I never left."

"Justin was the same; he lives and breathes the sport, but it was different for him – he almost didn't have a choice growing up, but you... you must have been born for it, to find your way to this level with no support from your family."

"I could say the same about you." I squeeze her hand. "You're the best physio I've ever had."

She giggles. "You're hardly going to say I'm the worst."

I chuckle. "No, I'm serious, my body is my livelihood – I don't just let anyone put their hands on it."

She dips her head before bringing her eyes back up to mine. "Well thank you for trusting me."

I *do* trust her; I realise in that moment. I've let her get close, right into my circle and I barely even noticed the intrusion.

Considering the small amount of people I let into that circle, it's a surprising revelation.

We walk down the quiet street, hand in hand not saying a word for nearly two blocks.

"Thanks for taking care of me, champ."

"You still gonna call me champ if I lose one day?"

She smiles at me. "I can't imagine you losing anytime soon, so I think you're safe."

"Everyone loses sometimes. Even me."

"Well, you'll always be my champ." She giggles and covers her eyes with her free hand as though she can't believe she just said something so cheesy.

I chuckle and do my best to swallow my feelings.

I want to be more than just her champ.

I want to be her everything.

"And you'll always be my pinky," I tell her.

"What if I change the colour of my hair?"

I shake my head. "It won't matter. It's stuck."

I can see the blush on her cheeks, even out here in the dim light.

I glance up and we're nearly at her street.

My time is almost up.

She gives me a forced smile, and I let myself believe that it's because she doesn't want me to leave any more than I do.

We turn the corner, still holding hands. This is so reckless, but I'm just doing what I do best – throwing everything I have into the ring.

"So... thanks for walking me, you didn't have to," she says as we walk up the short path to her front door.

"There was no way I was letting you walk alone."

We're dawdling, the pair of us, I don't know about her, but I'm dragging this thing out as long as I possibly can.

She turns to face me when we've got nowhere else to go.

She gives me a small smile and slightly pops one of her shoulders as if to say, 'what now?'

"I forgot, I got you something," I say, my memory sparking.

"*Me*? What for?"

I shrug. "Because I saw it and I wanted you to have it."

I shove my hand in my pocket and come back out with the small pink silk bag between my fingers.

I bring our joined hands up and let go so I can drop it in her hand.

She looks at me in confusion.

"Open it."

She pulls on the small string and tips it upside down, the small, gold, boxing glove charm falling into her palm.

Her eyes rise to mine. "*Hudson...*"

"It's for your bracelet."

"It's perfect, but *why*?"

"I thought I should have some type of representation."

She huffs out a laugh. "But why? Why *me*?"

I take a step closer to her. "I don't see anything around me when I'm in that cage – but I saw you, I saw you before I had any idea who you were... isn't that reason enough?" I rasp as I tuck her hair behind her ear, my other arm coming around her waist.

She nods slowly, her teeth sinking into her bottom lip.

I use my thumb to free it, and when I finally press my lips against hers, it's the rightest thing in the world.

CHAPTER FOURTEEN

Ramsey

There's something in the way I know he could literally snap me like a twig, yet he's handling me with such care and tenderness, that gets me – weakens my self-control to the point where I can't even remember why we *shouldn't* do this.

His lips are moving against mine with such softness and affection that I could cry.

He's *treasuring* me.

The hand that isn't gripping the sweet gift he just gave me, winds into his hair and holds on for dear life.

I feel weak in the knees, like I might fall down if he lets me go, and this time it has nothing to do with blood and everything to do with him.

He's making me dizzy.

I tug hard on his hair as I feel his tongue run across my lip.

He kisses me firmer – more urgently and I open my mouth to his.

I feel my back hit the wall next to my front door, but I can't even recall moving my feet.

He growls, and it's a deeply satisfied sound as I devour him the same way he does me until we both have to come up for air.

"Do you have any idea how long I've been waiting to do that?" he asks between planting kisses on my nose, cheeks and neck.

I don't know about him, but I've been waiting ever since the day I first met him, since I first saw his beautiful dark eyes and his smokin' hot body.

"About three weeks, six days, and I dunno, two hours?" I breathe.

He glances down at his watch. "And twenty-five minutes to be exact."

Our breaths mingle in the cool night air between us.

He's over-thinking, I can tell in the way he dips his head to stare at his shoes.

"Come inside," I whisper.

His face comes back to mine, and I run my hands down his chest and back up under his shirt, revelling in every glorious inch of his bare abdomen.

He groans and his head falls forward.

"You're making it really hard to do the right thing and walk away from you."

"So, don't walk away... I want you to stay, Hudson. Stay with me."

He doesn't say yes, but he doesn't say no either.

He watches as I slip my hand into my pocket and pull out my house key.

I unlock the door and take a step inside and set down the key and charm on the small table in the entry.

I look back at him from where I stand.

This is it.

This is his moment to do or die... to choose where his priorities lie.

He looks right at me, his dark eyes burning with desire as he steps surely over the threshold.

He made his choice.

I certainly made mine.

The moment he kissed me, I no longer had one.

He shuts the door behind him and steps into my body so we're pressed up against one another again. "Juliet made me promise I wouldn't break your heart," he murmurs.

I giggle nervously as I fidget with the end of my sleeve. "I don't know what goes through that girl's head sometimes."

He doesn't laugh. Instead he stares hard, seeing into the depths of my soul, then leans in and runs the tip of his nose from my ear to my throat.

"I won't break your heart if you don't break mine," he says, his voice gruff at my ear, and I melt into him.

I don't know who I think I'm fooling. He might not own my heart yet, but he's undoubtedly the one holding the strings.

"Deal," I whisper.

He kisses along my collar bone and down to the swell of my breasts. I go weak in the knees all over again.

"If you're going to kiss me like that, you might have to hold me up." My voice comes out like a moan as he nips and kisses my skin.

"I'm going to do *so* much more than that, Ramsey," he says, his eyes coming back up to meet mine.

They're a promise, those words.

This boy is going to steal my heart, I can feel it – I just have to pray that he keeps his word and doesn't break it to pieces once he has it in his hands.

We both know he's capable of destroying anything. Even me, that's if my brother doesn't kill me first once he finds out what's gone on here tonight.

Shit.

Hudson's still staring at me, and for a moment I think he might really be able to read my mind, because his gaze softens, and his hand reaches up and brushes the stray strands of hair from my face before gripping my chin between his thumb and finger.

"It's only us," he whispers. "Just you and me, pinky."

Fuck the consequences. Fuck the rules. I'd give up just about anything right now for it to be just me and him.

"It's only us," I reply as I tug his face to mine, our lips coming together in a flurry of passion and heat.

I'm backed up against a wall, one of my legs hitched around his hip before I can even take another breath.

"Hudson," I moan as he pulls his jacket off and lets it fall to the floor.

"Lift up," he growls as he tugs on the hem of my jersey.

I do as he asks, and he pulls it over my head, taking my shirt with it.

He tosses them over his shoulder, his eyes never leaving my body.

He takes his time, his gaze lazily roaming over my now only bra-covered chest as his fingers make quick work of the button on my jeans.

He leaves them on but undone, and I take the opportunity to rid him of his t-shirt.

I let my fingers roam over his toned torso the way I've wanted to every single time he's laid on my treatment bed.

I explore every groove and every ridge of his muscles until his head falls forward and he groans.

"You're barely even touching me and I feel weak."

"I know what you mean," I breathe as his lips meet the skin on my neck again.

His fingers skim down my bare sides and I feel goose bumps tingling in their wake.

"Take me to my room," I whisper.

He reaches around me and lifts me effortlessly into his arms, our fronts pressed together and my legs around his hips.

He walks us, his eyes never once leaving mine, through the living room and down the hallway to my bedroom.

The guy's got skills; we don't bump into a single thing.

"This is my room," I state lamely when he sits down on the edge of my bed, with me in his lap.

"I know, I looked in here when you were in the bathroom once."

"You snooped around my room, champ?" I grin.

He chuckles. "I did, and I'm not even sorry about it."

I run my hands up the back of his head, past the closely shaven section and into the longer hair on the top.

I could touch him like this all day.

"I can't believe this is finally happening. I've wanted you so bad."

I nod in agreement, words getting caught in my throat. I don't know how to process the fact that *he* wants *me*. I know he really does, I can feel how hard he is.

I doubt there's a woman in the world who would turn him down, but he's here with me – not with anyone else.

That knowledge makes me feel powerful.

"You're so pretty," he says and laughter bubbles from my throat.

The word sounds *wrong* coming from his mouth.

"Too cute?" He smirks.

"Way too cute... but I like it."

"You're the sexiest fucking woman I've ever laid eyes on," he growls as he flips me with ease so I'm on my back on the bed and he's hovering above me.

I gasp at the look in his dark eyes. It's primal – feral even.

It's hot as hell.

"That better?" he growls.

I nod, eyes wide.

He chuckles darkly, his lips turning up into a grin.

He pushes back so he's standing at the end of the bed, watching me as he undoes the button and fly of his dark jeans.

He shoves them down his legs, and I almost moan at the sight of him in his grey Calvin Klein's, looking powerful as hell and sexy as sin.

I don't think I've ever seen someone look so good, and I've spent a lot of time on Google images.

Every inch of him is toned to perfection. He's put back on the weight he lost before his last fight and his muscles are full and defined.

"You like the view?" he asks, a smirk pulling at the corner of his mouth.

"*Like* is an understatement," I murmur.

He chuckles and drops forward, his hands landing on either side on my hips.

He hooks his thumbs into the sides of my jeans and tugs them down my legs.

I've never felt so exposed in my entire life.

I've had sex with a handful of guys, but none that have looked at my body the way Hudson is – like he wants to worship every inch of it.

I've got a feeling that tonight is going to teach me the difference between men and boys.

"Seriously, Ramsey, you're so fucking beautiful."

His words, his tone, the look in his eye… he's the perfect mix of sweet and scary.

His fingers graze the lace of my underwear, and I have to hold back a moan.

This is too much, too intense and we haven't even got started yet.

He's barely touched me, and I'm *so* turned on.

He chuckles, the bastard knows exactly what he's doing to me.

I push up to my elbows and reach down with one hand, stroking his hard length from base to tip through his boxer briefs.

I swear his eyes roll back in his head.

"You're not laughing now, are you?" I smirk.

He presses my shoulder down, forcing me back onto the bed before settling between my legs.

He thrusts his hips and presses against me in the most delicious way.

"I need you, Hudson," I moan.

I've never needed anything more.

He dips his head to my ear and tugs the lobe into his mouth all the while continuing to grind his dick against me.

I feel my nails digging in, one hand on his back and the other in his hair.

His hand slips between us and I feel him tug.

The fucker just ripped my brand-new underwear.

"Those were new," I say, my voice coming out breathy and light instead of firm like I intended.

"I'll buy you a new pair," he mumbles against my neck.

He brings his mouth to mine at the same time I feel his fingers slip inside me.

"Jesus, Ramsey," he groans, his tone pained.

Something inside me snaps and I reach for his underwear, I shove at the band and he helps me get them free.

"Condoms in the top drawer," I whisper.

He reaches across the bed, still inside me, driving me *insane.*

I almost whimper as he slips his fingers out of me to slide on the condom, but when he replaces them with his hard length, I can't find a single thing to complain about.

CHAPTER FIFTEEN

Hudson

I just had my way with my best friend's little sister, and I know damn well it won't be the last time.

I don't want to think about what kind of mate that makes me.

She's staring at me with those beautiful golden eyes, worrying her bottom lip between her teeth.

She's thinking about the implications of this the same way I am.

We crossed a line tonight; one we can't just hop back over.

Things are different now.

"Penny for your thoughts?" she offers.

I feel my lips curving up into a smile – I can't seem to help it when she's around. I've never felt so content.

"Honestly?"

She nods.

"I was thinking about Justin and what's going to happen next."

Her eyes fall. "Me too."

"Hey, look at me." I tip her chin, so she has to look me right in the eyes. "We both knew what doing this was going to mean, but you're worth it, Ramsey, no matter what happens."

"But he's your best friend."

"And you're ..."

My soul mate.

The love of my life.

The most significant person I've ever met.

My other half.

"You're really important to me, pinky," I settle on saying.

"You're important to me too," she sighs, "but what if—"

"No *what ifs*," I cut her off. "Not tonight. We'll have time for that tomorrow."

"Okay," she whispers.

"It's still only us," I promise her, even though I'm pretty sure I heard Juliet get home about a half hour ago.

She smiles and leans in for a kiss, and yeah, I was dead right – I'm *definitely* going to have her again.

***

I hear my phone ring and I blink a couple of times against the harsh morning light.

I've got no clue what time it is, but judging by the sun streaming into this room, I'd say it's close to midday.

I glance down at Ramsey, her head on my shoulder and her eyes still peacefully closed.

I slip out from underneath her and try my best not to wake her – it's the least I can do after having her up so late.

I find my phone in the pocket of my jeans, thrown on the other side of her bedroom.

There's no sign of my shirt or jacket and I wince when I realise, they're still probably out by the front door for anyone who walks in to see.

I hope like fuck that Justin hasn't been to visit.

I unlock the screen and see six missed calls, one from Rusty and five from Justin, spanning from last night until this morning.

"Shit," I mutter.

It's eleven-thirty in the morning.

I don't know how the hell I'm going to cover this one up, if I haven't already been caught out, that is.

My car is sitting right outside her house, and if I'm right, a collection of my clothes are scattered through her house.

I run a hand through my hair.

I hit 'call back' on Justin's missed call and glance back at Ramsey, she's still sleeping.

I tip toe out of the room into the hallway and leave her door ajar behind me.

"Horror, where the fuck have you been?"

I rake a hand over my face. I can't lie and say I'm at home, because for all I know, that's where he is.

"I'm over at Ramsey's," I reply.

"You're back there already?"

I scrunch up my face as I weigh up my options. "Nah, I never left."

He's deathly silent.

Fuck.

I don't know what to do. I can't tell him this over the phone, and especially not without consulting Ramsey first.

That only leaves me with one other option – lie to him.

"We watched a movie when we got home, and I crashed out on the couch pretty late – I guess she left me there. I just woke up." The bullshit flows from my lips.

"You ditched a fight night to watch a movie with my sister?"

"Well I was hardly going to bring her back in so she could just faint again, was I?"

He's quiet for another few beats, and I run my hand through my hair again. I'm freaking out. I think he knows I'm lying.

"Is there something going on between you and Ramsey?"

"No."

Yes.

"We're friends."

We're *so much* more than friends.

"You told me to look out for her like she was my sister, so that's what I'm doing."

I almost gag on the words as they come out.

I don't think of Ramsey as a sister, not even one little bit.

"If you sleep with her, I'll kill you, you know that, right?"

I drop my forehead against the wall.

"What do you think is going on? That we're going to sleep together, fall in love and run off into the sunset? Not going to fucking happen. It's *me*; you know that's not going to happen."

Lies. So many lies.

I hear a noise behind me, but when I turn around and peek through the gap, Ramsey is still sleeping soundly in her bed.

"Alright," he replies, satisfied.

I blow out a breath. "What do you want anyway?"

"Just checking in – seeing where the hell you disappeared to."

"Well I'm right here..."

We talk about the results from the fights I missed before agreeing to meet at the gym in the morning for training.

I hang up the call and listen down the hallway for any signs of life.

I can't hear anyone, so I stalk down to the living room, collecting clothes as I go.

I'm sure Juliet has seen them already, but before anyone else does, they're coming with me.

I slip back into Ramsey's room and shut the door behind me.

Her eyes are still closed, and I can't help but smile even though everything is a mess.

Shit is going to get all fucked up with Justin when this comes out. He's going to hate me. Rusty and Beast will probably hate me on his behalf too.

I wouldn't even blame them.

I shove my feet into my jeans and yank them up. I've got a meeting at one with Owen to go over my nutrition for the next few weeks and then Randy wants to show me a few clips of my floor work from my last bout and see where he thinks we can improve.

I've got to go home and shower, eat, and get back downtown to the gym in an hour and a half.

I sit down on Ramsey's side of the bed and sweep some of her pink hair from her face.

She's so fucking beautiful.

"Pinky," I whisper as I shake her shoulder gently.

Her eyes open slowly. "Hey," she whispers, her voice unsure.

I know how she feels; I felt the same way when I watched her sleep just now, but we'll figure something out.

We have to.

"I have to shoot off, I've got a meeting at one."

"What's the time?" she asks, her voice thick with sleep.

"Half eleven."

"Okay," she says, and I can hear something in her voice that makes me feel sad for some reason.

I lean down and kiss her forehead. "I'll call you later, okay?"

She nods, and I swear I can see tears catching in her lashes.

"Are you alright?"

She smiles, but it doesn't quite reach her eyes. "I'm good, go, you'll be late."

I stand and shrug on my shirt and jacket I rescued from near the front door.

I pause by the door to her room.

Jesus, what the hell is wrong with me... I miss her already.

I glance back at her and her eyes are closed again.

I turn the door handle and do my best to push aside the feeling that something is wrong.

CHAPTER SIXTEEN

Ramsey

I run to the window and watch as he drives off down the street in his fast, expensive car.

The tears I was holding in so tight spill down my cheeks.

I feel so stupid.

Here I was, *falling*. Thinking this was something real between us.

"What do you think is going on? That we're going to sleep together, fall in love and run off into the sunset? Not going to fucking happen. It's me, you know that's not going to happen."

I don't know who he was talking to, but the message was clear.

It's not going to fucking happen.

Everything I've fantasised about and after last night, believed was possible, came crashing down around me after I heard him speak those words.

I'm such a fool.

My phone beeps with a new message and I grab it off my nightstand as I climb back into bed and the safety of my covers.

My hand shakes as I see his name on my screen.

To: Ramsey

From: Hudson
I miss you already, pinky.

I laugh bitterly and hit the power button, turning it off before tossing it onto the bed.

Hudson Scott may have fooled me once, but it won't happen again.

No matter how much I might want it to.

I can still feel where he touched my skin, where he's been inside me.

Another tear slides down my cheek.

I feel so used.

He played me and he won.

I guess I said it myself. He *always* wins.

There's a soft knock at my door and I swipe away the moisture from my face.

"Ramsey?" Juliet asks gently. "I can hear you crying..."

I huff out a laugh, but it comes out croaky and wet sounding.

"Can I come in?"

"Yeah." I bury my head in the pillow so she can't see how pathetic I am.

"What's wrong?"

I feel the bed dip as she sits down in the same spot Hudson sat in only a few minutes earlier.

The thought has tears welling up in my eyes all over again.

I don't answer.

"What the fuck did he do? Ramsey, you *never* cry."

She's right. I don't cry, but this... it hurts.

"Ramsey!" she demands when I still don't answer.

"How'd you know he was here?" I ask.

"You mean beside the fact that there was a trail of your clothes leading to the bedroom and his car was parked out front all night?"

"Shit."

She nods in agreement. "You're just lucky Justin was content to walk me to my car and didn't insist on following me back here."

I don't feel very lucky right now. I just gave my heart and my body to a man who doesn't even want it.

"Everything is a mess."

"Do you want to talk about it?"

I shake my head, then change my mind and nod.

I don't know *what* I want, but I do know one thing, I can't figure this out on my own, so I spill and tell my best friend everything from the boxing glove charm to the phone call I heard half of this morning.

"What the fuck?" she demands.

I shrug.

"What a dick move."

"Right?"

"Kinda seems out of character though..."

"I heard the words come from his mouth, Jules." I groan.

"But he text you and said he missed you..."

"So maybe he enjoys messing with my head?"

"Maybe you were never meant to hear that phone call?"

"Clearly I wasn't." I sigh. "But that doesn't change the fact that I *did*."

"True." She frowns.

"I don't know, Ramsey, something doesn't add up. That guy is *obsessed* with you, I don't believe that he doesn't want something more... why don't you just talk to him about it... tell him what you heard?"

"I don't know if I can," I whisper. "I've fallen for him, Jules, and if he doesn't want the same things I do, it's going to crush me."

She reaches for my hand and squeezes it gently.

"What's the alternative? Never talk to him again?"

I shrug. "I don't know... I just need some time to think about it."

She nods in understanding. "Fair enough."

I grab a pillow and throw it over my face.

"Is it awkward if I ask how the sex was? Because shit, that man looks like he's made for it."

I tug the pillow from my face and smack her with it, a grin trying to find its way onto my face despite my heartbreak.

He was made for it alright; as confused and hurt as I am – there's absolutely no doubt about that.

"I'm *not* talking about him like that."

"You're right. It's too soon." She giggles. "I'll give you a few days to recover."

She gets up off my bed and heads for the door. "So just to clarify, you're going to be ignoring him until further notice?"

"Yes please," I say, my voice muffled from the pillow that has taken up residence across my face again.

"So what do I do when he turns up here?"

"He won't."

"Oh, sweetie, trust me... he will."

"Then tell him I'm sick or something... I don't care, just don't let him in."

"Are you sure that's what you want?"

I sigh. "I have no fucking idea."

"Want me to go out and get some ice cream?"

"I love you."

She huffs out a laugh. "I know you do."

I poke my head out from its hiding spot and call after her, "I'll love you even more if you get me cookies and cream flavour."

I hear her laugh and then the front door opening and closing.

I reach for my phone so I can read his message a second time but pull my hand back when I remember that I turned it off, and that I'm taking a minute to think this through.

I'm destined to fail. I'm addicted to him, as much as I don't want to be.

I groan and fall back to the soft pillows.

Running the risk of sounding like Taylor Swift, I knew he was trouble when he walked in – I just wish I could have had the good sense to listen to myself.

***

"I feel sick, you shouldn't have let me eat all of that."

"What do you expect me to do?" Juliet questions, a spoon hanging from her hand. "You probably would have bit me if I tried to take that away from you."

We've done nothing but watch trashy chick flicks all afternoon, and dutifully ignore my still-turned-off cell that's sitting in the centre of the coffee table in front of me.

It's killing me – not knowing if he's tried to call or text.

"You going to switch that thing on or not? You can't hide forever."

"I'm not sure a few hours counts as forever."

She rolls her eyes. "Suit yourself, but if you don't let him know you're alive, I'm pretty sure he's going to show up here looking for you."

I don't know that he will, not unless he's worried I might spill my guts to Justin, but maybe she's right and I should just flick him a text...

She gets to her feet. "I have to pee."

She slides the phone purposefully in my direction and leaves the room.

I stare at it for what feels like forever before grabbing it and powering it up.

It's been about seven hours since he left, so if there's no missed calls or texts from him – that'll be answer enough.

My screen comes to life and I chew on my fingernails.

It dings, one, two, three, four times.

My heart starts to thump in my chest.

There are three missed calls – two from Hudson, and one from Justin, and one message.

My pulse rockets into overdrive at the possibility that Justin already knows.

I click on the little message button and release a deep breath when I read it. The text is from Justin – he sent it after I didn't answer his call.

To: Ramsey
    From: Justin
    Am I allowed to beat up your patient yet or what?

He doesn't know.

I go back to the call log to see when Hudson called.

There's one from around three this afternoon and another from only about twenty minutes ago.

I know he had a busy afternoon at the gym today – so if I had to guess, he's called me between sessions and then now, when he's done for the day.

What he wanted to say though, that is still a mystery.

I decide to send a text to him.

To: Hudson
    From: Ramsey
    Sorry I missed your call, I'm not feeling well – going to hit the hay. Night.

It's not a total lie – I can feel my stomach curdling, from all the ice cream or the situation I've found myself in, I'm not sure.

I go back to Justin's message and think about what I want to reply.

I know what I need to do.

Hudson and I have been dragging his treatment out for far longer than it needed anyway. He's ready to get back into training, and if he's back training then he'll have no reason to turn up here twice a week – and maybe that would be the easiest for both of us.

To: Justin

From: Ramsey

He's good to go – treatment is finished, I'm officially discharging him into your care. Try not to break him on the first day.

I let my head fall back against the couch and blow out a deep breath through my nose.

"Did you text him?" Juliet asks from behind me.

I slowly open my eyes and make the decision to turn off my phone again.

I nod as the screen turns black.

"I told him I wasn't feeling well and was going to bed."

"*Ramsey...*" she groans.

"Just leave it, Jules, I'll figure it all out tomorrow. Right now, I'm going to actually go to bed – it's been a long few hours."

She smiles sadly at me as I get to my feet and retreat down the hallway.

I consider changing my sheets, but as soon as my head hits the pillow and I smell his masculine scent, I don't have the will power to get back up.

CHAPTER SEVENTEEN

Hudson

I glance at the time on the big wall clock.

I know it's early for a Monday, but Ramsey usually starts with clients at eight, so I expected to have heard from her by now.

She was acting so strange last night – her message came through while I was showering, and by the time I read it and tried to call, her phone was turned off again.

Same thing this morning.

If I wasn't meeting Justin here, I would have swung by her place to see if she was okay.

She said she wasn't feeling well – I hope it's nothing serious.

"Morning, pretty boy, you ready to get your ass kicked?" Justin taunts me as he strolls across the gym.

I chuckle. "Hate to rain on your parade, but I haven't got the all clear."

His face stretches into a wide grin. "Ramsey didn't tell you?"

Didn't tell me what...

"You've been discharged, man, you're good to get back to training."

"She must have forgot to tell me." I frown.

I don't like this.

Ramsey and I have spoken nearly every day since my last fight, we've talked about everything and anything, and now, right after we sleep together, I'm getting messages via her brother.

Something isn't right.

"Glove up, I'm going to put you through the wringer." He claps me on the shoulder as he strolls past, his gear bag slung over his shoulder.

I watch him disappear from sight into the changing rooms and I snag my phone from my own bag.

I hit dial on her name and it goes straight to voicemail again.

"Fuck," I mutter under my breath.

I toss it back in the bag and run my hand through my hair in frustration.

"You're looking soft, Horror, I'm going to make you my bitch," Justin's voice calls from the changing room.

I'll have to figure out what to do about Ramsey later.

I grab my hand wraps and start to wind them around my knuckles. Right now, I have to deal with her pain-in-the-ass brother.

***

"Not bad. I'm surprised you're not more wrecked." Justin pants, his hands resting on his knees as he doubles over.

I slump onto the bench and suck in a deep breath.

I don't know what the hell he's looking at, I *am* wrecked.

My lungs are burning and my muscles are screaming in protest.

Twelve rounds straight with a guy like him is no walk in the park.

I can feel a few new bruises coming up – nothing too serious given the shin guards and sixteen-ounce gloves we sparred in, but still enough to leave a mark.

Everything leaves a mark in this sport.

I spit my mouth guard into my glove and deposit it into my bag, then begin tugging the gloves off.

It's days like these, when you can feel it, even when you're being hit with these big gloves for cushioning, that you realise how unconditioned your body is.

A month off feels like a year all of a sudden.

I need to get back into my training with Owen – work on my conditioning.

"Your uppercut is still shit house," Justin says through sucking in air.

I squirt a stream of water into my mouth, most of it dripping down my front.

"That's not what you were saying when I caught you on the jaw."

"I wouldn't say it was 'shit house' but it could use some work," a voice from the left says.

"Oh hey, Dad, I didn't know you were in already."

"Caught the last two rounds," Joseph Ashton tells his son as he reaches us.

"Good to see you, Joe." I hold out my now un-gloved hand to him and he shakes it firmly.

It's been a while since I've seen Joe – he'd been away with fighters prior to my last bout, and I've made my presence scarce around here since then.

"You look better out of shape than half the guys around here look *in* shape, son," he tells me with a nod.

"Well I feel like shit."

He laughs lightly. "Nothing quite as shitty as feeling out of shape."

Not hearing from his daughter well and truly trumps it, but I don't feel like dying today, so I'm not about to tell him that.

"When's your next fight?" he questions, and I glance up at Justin.

He shrugs. "Nothing on the cards for the next six months."

"Something will pop up, it always does – some fool will decide he wants to take a belt from you, and it'll be all on."

"Don't go putting stupid ideas in his head," Justin groans. "We don't need another title fight for a while yet."

Joe glances across the gym at the sound of people entering.

"The youth academy is here, I gotta go."

We say our goodbyes, and then it's just the two of us at the side of the vacant ring again.

I can hear Joe barking orders at the young guys, and I see the kid I sponsored in there with them.

"How's he doing?" I nod my head at the ginger-haired young guy.

"Good, man, good, really good actually – future champ in the making I reckon."

The word 'champ' hits me right in the gut.

Something isn't right with Ramsey, I can feel it.

"When did you talk to your sister?" I ask casually as I unwind my now sweat-covered hand wraps.

"Last night." He grunts, the Velcro on his shin guards sounding as he undoes the straps.

"I think I left a jersey around there, I might shoot round and grab it."

He grunts again.

I rip off my own shin guards and toss everything into the huge bag that seems to go everywhere with me.

"Tell her I might need to see her after today."

I smirk at him as I lace up my shoes.

"Pussy."

He flips me the middle finger.

"Go for a run later – just light, about an hour or so should do it," he instructs.

"Will do." I nod as I get to my feet and sling my bag over my shoulder.

"You not hitting the showers?" he questions.

I shake my head. "Nah, might head out for that run when I get home... just get it done," I lie.

I won't run until later, the only reason I'm not showering now is because I want to get to Ramsey's place sooner.

"Whatever does it for you, man."

"I'll catch you tomorrow?"

He nods as he clutches his side.

I chuckle, so much for him kicking my ass.

I slide into my car and try Ramsey once more, but she still isn't answering.

I know the speed limit, but I ignore it as I drive over to her house.

I feel panicked, on edge for some reason, and I don't like it.

I park outside her place and jog up the path.

I stink and I'm pretty sure I've got a black eye forming, but there's no blood, so I figure I'm safe.

I rap my knuckles on the door and listen.

I hear feet moving towards the door.

I can see her car parked in the driveway, so I know she's here.

She swings open the door and just the sight of her takes my breath away and settles the feeling that has been swirling in my gut for the past eighteen or so hours.

"*Ramsey.*"

"Hudson... you're not my nine o'clock," she replies.

She doesn't look sick. Not even a little bit.

I shake my head at her. "Nope, *apparently* I've been given the all clear."

I don't mean it to come out like an accusation, but it does.

Blush stains her cheeks and she shifts nervously from one foot to the other. "Look, can we do this later? My client will be here any minute."

I cross my arms firmly across my chest and ignore her request. "You're ignoring my calls. Why?"

She shrugs one of her shoulders. "I'm not ignoring you, Hudson, I just don't know what I'm meant to say."

She tucks a strand of pink hair behind her ear and dips her head, trying to hide the tears I can see welling in her eyes.

"Hey," I say, my voice softening. "Did I do something wrong?"

She looks back up at me, her lashes wet. "You tell me."

I frown. "Is this about Justin?"

She shakes her head.

I reach for her arm, but she shifts slightly so I can't make contact.

My hand falls and my stomach turns.

"Pinky, I don't know what happened between now and then, but Saturday night was..."

"It was a mistake," she cuts me off and it feels like a knife has just been driven into my heart.

"A mistake," I deadpan.

I can't believe she just said that. That night wasn't a mistake in the slightest. It was everything I wanted and more.

"I really have to go," she whispers.

"So that's it then?" I shrug. "You're ghosting me?"

She shakes her head, sadness filling her eyes. "No. I'm letting you off the hook."

I don't want to be off the fucking hook.

"This could never work between us," She shrugs. "You and Justin – you're like brothers... I can't come between you two like that, and you wouldn't want that either. He's important to you. You can't just throw that away for me."

It's bullshit. The whole lot of this is bullshit.

This isn't her decision to make for me.

"If you don't want this, you can just say so, Ramsey, don't dress it up and try and make it seem like you're doing something noble."

My words hit her, and she looks as though she might physically buckle under them.

"I think you should go," she whispers.

I nod my head once and do what she wants me to.

I leave.

CHAPTER EIGHTEEN

Ramsey

"I'm cutting you off," Juliet says, her voice full of authority.

I look up at her and drop my bottom lip.

She's got her hands on her hips and a scowl on her face. She means business.

"You've eaten your body weight in ice cream since that night and it stops *now*. You'll end up lactose intolerant for fuck's sake."

"It makes me feel better."

I groan as she snags the tub of ice cream from on the couch cushion where I've got it sitting – a spoon stuck out of the top.

"It does not," she mutters as she stalks back to the kitchen with it. "It makes you feel bloated and gross."

She's right. It does.

I swear I've put on five kilos this past week.

"The only thing that's going to make you feel better," she informs me as she appears back in the living room, "is going and talking to Hudson and putting all your fucking cards on the table, because you are seriously miserable right now."

"It's got nothing to do with him," I try and lie.

She laughs humourlessly. "Don't start that shit with me, it has *everything* to do with him, and that's exactly why I'm driving you over there so you can talk to him."

"I can drive myself, you know. I have a license... and a car."

"I know you do." She raises her brows at me. "But what happened on Wednesday when I sent you over there?"

My brow furrows and I pout. "I went to McDonald's for an hour."

"Exactly."

"It could have been worse, I could have gone somewhere that didn't have free WiFi."

She rolls her eyes at me.

"Get dressed."

I cross my arms and legs stubbornly.

"Fine. Go looking like trailer trash, see if I care – but you're going. I don't care if I have to call Justin or Rusty over here to lift you into the car – I'll do it," she threatens me.

Shit.

She's not even kidding.

"*Fine*," I hiss. "I'll get dressed."

"Good." She smirks in satisfaction. "And brush your hair or something, you look like one of those candyfloss sticks you get at a carnival."

I flip her off, but when I get into my room and glance in the mirror, it's actually a fair representation.

I tug my brush through the knotty mess and throw on some clothes that should pass her inspection.

She's still waiting for me when I get back to the living room, only now her car keys are in her hand.

"Let's go."

***

The drive over there feels like it takes *forever*. There are nerves going crazy in my belly.

I don't know what I'm going to say to him – 'I'm miserable without you in my life' is probably going to sound pretty pathetic.

"Stop jiggling your knee, it's driving me *insane*," Juliet demands as we round the final corner and find ourselves on Hudson's street.

"Sorry," I whisper.

She pulls up outside his house and I look up at the lit up windows.

"It looks like he has company, we should come back tomorrow."

"It's just Justin and the guys," she says, pointing to the driveway where Justin, Rusty and Beast have all parked their vehicles. "Justin told me they were coming over to play video games tonight."

"Well that's settled then. I can't talk to him in front of Justin."

She rolls her eyes. "That's why I'm here, sunshine. I'll go hang out with the guys, and you can go talk to that scary man you're so fond of."

I feel the corner of my mouth twitch into a smile. "He's not actually all that scary."

That's just a front for the world – to keep them somewhat at bay so he can live the life he wants – fight – but not get dragged into any media bullshit.

She opens her door. "Whatever you say, now, shall I send him out, or are you coming in?"

There's no way I'm going to make even more of a loser of myself by staying in the car.

I open my door, and she grins triumphantly.

We walk side by side towards the house in silence. I can hear music coming from inside. It sounds like a lot more than a few video games.

"Are you sure they're not having a party?"

She shrugs. "Not that I'm aware of."

We reach the front door and Juliet gives me a little shove. "Hurry up and knock already."

"Jeeze, calm down," I grumble as I raise my hand and knock loudly on the wooden door.

My heart thumps in my chest, but nothing happens.

They can't hear me over the music.

"They can't hear, let's just go."

I turn and try to slip past her, but she's not having any of it.

"Not so fast, chicken shit."

She tries the handle, but the door is locked.

"Uh huh," she announces victoriously as she spots and presses the door bell off to the side.

The bell sounds loudly through the house, and I hang my head in defeat. They're *definitely* going to have heard that.

The volume of the music lowers and I hear feet approaching the door.

My heart rate speeds up again. I don't know if I'm ready for this – to come face to face with the man I *shouldn't* want, but one hundred percent do.

The door swings open and I hear myself gasp.

This is not who I was expecting to see.

"Can I help you?" Vanessa asks, her brow cocked arrogant-ly.

She's standing there in his doorway, acting like the lady of the house and all of a sudden, I feel like I might be sick.

I torture myself, letting my eyes look her over from head to toe – she's a bitch, you can tell from the look in her eye, but she's also gorgeous.

"Is Hudson here?" Juliet asks her politely.

"*Yeah...* he's here," Vanessa replies, her lips curving into a sly grin.

"So can we speak to him or what?" Juliet demands and I give her a virtual high-five.

Vanessa narrows her eyes at me, and I know she remembers me from the last time I was here. I wish I knew why she was here again.

She turns, takes a few steps into the house and calls over her shoulder, "Horror, *someone* is here to see you."

Hudson appears behind her, shirtless – that sexy eagle tattoo spread wide across his chest, he's got a drink in one hand, a laugh is still falling from his lips.

Until his eyes land on me at least.

"Ramsey?" he breathes.

"Hey," I squeak, waving awkwardly.

Vanessa welds herself to his side, her arm snaking out to wrap around his waist. "Who is *she*, babe?"

I watch the action like it's happening in slow motion.

I try to swallow the lump in my throat, but I can't. I feel physically ill.

"I shouldn't have come," I whisper, and when I turn and push past Juliet, she doesn't even try to stop me this time.

This was a mistake. I should never have just turned up here like this.

I run down the path and I hear Hudson yelling my name, but I don't turn.

I reach the car and swing the door open just in time for his hand to come crashing down, slamming it shut again.

I've got my back pinned against the car door before I even register that he's there, one of his toned arms on either side of my head.

"*Ramsey*," he says, and his eyes search my face for a clue as to what the fuck I'm doing here. "Where do you think you're going?"

"I'm sorry," I stutter. "I can't stand there and talk to you while she's got her claws on you... I just *can't*."

He frowns at me. "Vanessa?" he questions.

I can't answer him without spinning into a jealous rage, so I say nothing.

I don't know why it hurts so much to see them together, but it does.

He had me, and then disregarded me. Maybe he does the same to her, I don't know, but I certainly don't want to see it.

My fucked-up heart has fallen for this man – as much as he doesn't deserve it.

"I should just go."

"You're not leaving until you tell me what you're doing here."

I hear a door slam and I peer around his arm to see that Juliet and bitch face are gone.

"I wanted to talk to you," I whisper as his dark, smouldering eyes drag my focus back to him.

He flexes and every muscle in his half-naked body tenses.

This is the first time he's ever really looked one hundred percent frightening to me.

I know he wouldn't hurt me, but I'm still afraid.

"*Now* you want to talk to me?" he demands.

I nod weakly.

"I called and called, Ramsey."

"I know," I whisper, I know because I ignored every single one, until they stopped coming. I didn't know what else to do.

"What the fuck happened?" he demands.

I feel the tears welling in my eyes. "You broke my heart," I practically yell at him.

"*I* broke *your* heart?" he growls. "*Me?*"

I nod, the drops of moisture sliding down my face now. "You promised you wouldn't and then you *did*."

"*You* blew *my* heart to smithereens!" he roars into the night, pushing off the car and running his hand through his hair in frustration. "Jesus Christ, Ramsey, what the fuck is this?"

I don't know what he's saying – none of this makes sense. All I know for sure is that he hurt me. He hurt me with his words when he didn't even know I could hear them.

I cling to that with all the strength I have.

"What did you think was going on between us? That we were going to sleep together, fall in love and run off into the sunset?" I throw the words that broke me, back at him like venom.

"Fuck this," he growls, stalking away.

"What do you care anyway, right? Plenty more where I came from."

He turns and steps back in my direction, then thinks better of it and paces back towards the house again.

"I'm sure Vanessa will be more than happy to fill the void."

I can't seem to stop. I can't make myself stop talking.

"She's *nothing* to me," he roars, facing me again, "a *leech*, a problem I can't get rid of. She. Is. Nothing."

"And I guess I'm nothing too," I whisper, my voice cracking under the weight of my emotions.

His dark eyes widen but I don't give him time to reply.

"I'm not doing this anymore. I can't. I'm done," I tell him, my voice empty and hollow.

I turn and start walking down the street into the dark night.

I don't know how long Juliet is going to be in there and I can't sit in the car and wait, or worse yet – stay out here arguing with him. My heart can't take it.

"Ramsey!" he calls after me. "Don't just walk away."

I swipe at the tears running uncontrollably down my cheeks, but I don't look at him as he continues yelling after me.

There's no going back now.

In the movies the guy always chases after the girl when she walks away from him.

This *definitely* isn't the movies – this is my sad, pathetic life, because when I walk away, he doesn't follow.

CHAPTER NINETEEN

Hudson

"Motherfucker!" I bellow into my yard, the curse echoing around the quiet street.

I punch a small tree and it snaps back, almost cracking in half.

This must be my karma for betraying my best mate, because *fuck* I'm hurting.

I don't know what the hell just went on here in my front yard, but it's the opposite of what I wanted to happen, and now she's out there in the darkness by herself.

I jog up to my door and throw it open, not even bothering to close it behind me.

Vanessa is lingering in the hallway, her eyes darting to me the instant I enter, before glancing behind me to see if I'm alone.

Her lips turn up into a grin when she sees I am.

I don't know what the fuck Beast was thinking bringing those chicks over here – Cassidy – the girl he's interested in is cool, and her other friend is alright too, but Vanessa – not so much.

She's been on me like a rash ever since she arrived and I'm sick to fucking death of it.

This is the last time she's going to fuck things up for me. She messed with Ramsey and that is not going to fly with me.

I point a warning finger at her as I storm past. "Wait there," I demand.

She salutes me, thinking she's hot as fucking shit, and it takes everything I have not to throw her out on her ass right now.

I can hear noise coming from upstairs, so I assume that's where everyone else is.

I stride up the stairs to my games room and take a deep breath before sticking my head around the door frame and looking around for Juliet.

She's right where I expect her to be, under one of Justin's arm.

The other two girls are sitting with Beast and Rusty – watching them play some car racing game I never got into.

It's like a fucking triple date in here.

"Hey, Jules, Ramsey isn't feeling well – can you drive her home?"

Justin glances up at me before shifting his gaze down to Juliet.

"I'll call you tomorrow."

She nods eagerly and slides out from her seat.

She steps away but he snags her hand, halting her.

He squeezes her hand and a look passes between them.

I know what that look means.

It reminds me of the way I feel when I see Ramsey.

Justin is screwed.

He drops her hand and she rushes from the room, blush-ing.

She slips past me and sits her hands on her hips as she glares at me.

"What the hell—"

"Shhh," I hiss at her.

I grab her arm and drag her into a spare room a few doors down.

She narrows her eyes at me and tugs her arm out of my hold.

"What did you do?" she demands.

"Honestly?" I ask, my hand running through me hair. "I've got no fucking idea, but we argued, and she stormed off."

Juliet's eyes widen.

"I'd have gone after her myself, but she'd be too stubborn to get in the car."

"So you just let her walk off into the night alone?"

"Can you yell at me later?" I plead. "Right now, I just need to know she's okay."

She looks like she wants to stand here and yell at me for five minutes, but she doesn't – she glares at me one last time and turns, storming out of the room and down the stairs.

"Don't let the door hit you on the way out, honey." I hear Vanessa giggle like the fucking bitch she is.

I don't know how I ever thought sleeping with that psycho was a good idea.

She's the reason I had a drink tonight in the first place – I thought if I had some alcohol thrumming in my veins that maybe she wouldn't be so painful to deal with.

I couldn't have been more wrong.

I had a drink – so she had a drink and that only made her more annoying.

I think I'd need to get hit by a truck to make this bitch any less painful.

I stalk across the living area, snagging her jacket from where she's tossed it over the back of the couch.

Her shoes are kicked off in two random spots of my living room – like she owns the damn place.

I scoop them up too and dump all her shit in a pile at her feet.

The smug smirk slowly falls from her lips. "What are you doing?"

"Taking out the trash."

Her eyes widen. "You're kicking me out? For what? *Her*?"

"Fuck yes for *her*. You crossed the line the second you looked at her with that evil fucking glint in your eye, so I'm doing what I should have done the minute you walked in – I'm kicking you out."

"You can't kick me out."

"Can't I?" I chuckle darkly. I'd like to see her try and stop me.

"My friends are upstairs."

"Does it look like I give a shit? Either you go up and get them, or you leave on your own."

Her mouth opens and closes like a goldfish, but nothing comes out.

"Beast!" I bellow up the stairs.

"Yeah?" he calls back.

"Vanessa needs to go, you ready to take off?"

"Be down in a sec," he replies.

I smirk at Vanessa as she looks on in shock, like she can't believe I'm really serious.

Justin appears on the stairs, everyone else coming down behind him.

"What's going on?" he asks me, sensing the tension between us instantly.

"She was being a bitch to Ramsey and Juliet," I tell him honestly.

Vanessa's eyes widen further.

Justin looks at her like the piece of scum she is.

"Get her out of here," I say lazily, turning away from her and strolling into my kitchen.

I don't give a shit who does the job, as long as it gets done.

Beast shoots me an apologetic glance, but it's not his fault. Vanessa is the problem here.

"Don't even think about coming within a two-mile radius of me again, Vanessa," I drawl as I hear everyone shuffling out the front door.

I hear a whimpering noise and I chuckle.

"About time you blacklisted that skank."

I flip the top off another beer and bring the bottle to my lips.

"She the reason Ramsey took off so quick?" he asks.

I glance at him. He looks worried for his sister.

I seriously consider telling him – the whole truth about what's going on.

Justin is the guy I go to if I've got women troubles, but I doubt he's going to be too forthcoming with advice if he knew that the only woman I want to talk about is his sister.

"I think that had something to do with it," I reply.

It's not a total lie at least.

I may not have a clue what we just fought about, but I know Vanessa being here tonight didn't help the situation in the slightest.

He eyes me curiously for a moment and I don't like it, it feels like he's seeing too much.

"I'm going to hit the road too," he tells me, slinging his thumb over his shoulder.

I nod. "I'll see you tomorrow?"

He tips his chin up at me. "Better make that your last beer, wouldn't want it to be too easy to beat you." He chuckles.

I shake my head and smirk at him.

He's so full of shit.

I listen as he leaves and then I'm all alone.

The hideous music Vanessa was playing has been shut off and it's airily quiet in here.

I make my way around the living room, collecting bottles, turning off lights and locking doors before going upstairs to do the same.

It's not until I'm in my room, *alone*, replaying everything Ramsey said to me tonight that it hits me.

Those were *my* words – not hers.

She heard me on the phone last week after we slept together.

Fucking hell.

Blood pounds in my ears as I think about the mistake I've made.

I've screwed *everything* up.

She was right.

It was *me* who broke *her* heart and I'm a total fucking wanker for it.

***

I pound the bag over and over again until my vision is blurry from the exertion.

"Whoa, whoa, whoa." I hear Justin behind me, his hands coming to rest on my shoulders and pulling me backwards. "You trying to wreck yourself?"

"Just letting off some steam." I grunt as I shrug him off.

I shift to leg work, throwing kicks and knees with all the strength I can muster.

I haven't got shin guards on, and I know I'll wind up leaving bruises using a bag this firm, but I don't care.

"One of those days, huh?" I hear him grumble as he tosses his gym bag to the floor.

He leaves me alone for a few minutes.

"Let's go then." I hear the familiar clap of the focus pads being smacked together.

I turn and he's layered up in protective gear.

"You want to beat the shit out of something? Come on then," he taunts me.

I shift my focus from the bag to him.

He grins at me. "Let me know when you're exhausted – then we'll jump in the ring... it'll make kicking your ass reeeealll easy."

I nod in agreement.

I might even let him beat me today – it's the least I deserve.

I advance on him, already in my fighting stance, and I hit him until I can't lift my arms and my legs are threatening to stop holding me up.

"Enough," he barks after what seems like an eternity.

I drop to the floor and suck in deep breath after deep breath.

He rips off the padding on his legs and around his middle and tosses it to the ground.

He tugs up his t-shirt and winces as he prods at his side. "You crazy bastard, I think you cracked one of my ribs."

I glance up at him and shrug. I'm too wrecked to speak.

He'll be alright. It's nothing he hasn't done to me over the years.

"What the fuck was that all about?"

I ignore him. Why I've got so much pent up aggression is the last thing I want to talk about right now.

I spot Randy across the gym, and he grins when he sees me in a heap on the floor.

"Getting back in shape, kid?" He chuckles as he looks between me and Justin, who is still trying to decide if he's broken something or not.

I nod, still desperately trying to suck air into my lungs.

"Good, you're going to need to be."

I want to ask him what that's meant to mean, but the words aren't coming out – I'm concerned if I open my mouth to try, I'll vomit.

"What do you want him in shape for?" Justin cuts in, saving me.

"He's been challenged." Randy grins.

Justin reaches into his gear bag and tosses me an electrolyte drink.

It hits me on the shoulder, and I reach for it, my arms shaking. There's no way in hell I was catching that.

I've pushed my body to its absolute limit in the past two and a half hours.

"Challenged by *who*?" Justin demands.

This is nothing new, but the excited look on Randy's face is.

He only gets excited when a big name comes knocking. "Sonny Perez."

Shit.

This *is* big.

The first half of my career, I fought as a lightweight – I hold the belt for that division. More recently I've stepped into the cage as a welterweight – about fifteen pounds heavier than I was.

Sonny is a champion middleweight fighter – another whole weight class up from me.

"He wants to challenge that shiny new belt."

Taking this fight wouldn't be a smart move on my behalf.

I'll come in just over the minimum weight and he'd scrap in right under the maximum.

We could stand in that cage with ten to fifteen pounds difference between us.

"No fucking way, get that stupid grin off your face, there is no way in fuck that we're going to—"

"Take it," I interrupt him, finding my voice.

A calm settles over me as I say the words, and I know then that there won't be any talking me out of this.

I need a distraction from Ramsey, and what better way than prepping for what could be the toughest fight of my career.

"Horror, he's coming down a weight class, he'll crush you."

"I'll put weight on."

"It won't help," Justin argues. "You know they're going to have you vacate that lightweight belt unless you drop back down for another fight soon – that's what we should be focusing on."

"I said, *take it*." I pin him with my stare, leaving no room for argument.

"Your fucking funeral," he mutters under his breath.

"For real?" Randy asks, his eyes dancing with anticipation.

"Call them. We'll take it." I nod.

"When are they talking?" Justin demands.

He might not like the idea at all, but he'll be there beside me, training me the whole way.

"In a month."

"That'll do." I nod at him.

"Jesus, Mary and Joseph." Justin smacks a focus pad down on the ground. "Are you on a suicide mission or something? You seriously want to fight *Sonny Perez* in four and half weeks' time?"

"I don't just *want* to," I say as I push to my feet and head for the showers. "I *am*."

CHAPTER TWENTY

Ramsey

Words like 'death wish', 'idiot', 'tough bastard' and 'suicide mission', ring in my ears.

Even Juliet can't calm Justin down this afternoon.

He's come over once a week for the past four weeks, ranting and raving, and normally nursing some type of injury that he needs me to treat for him.

Every time he comes to that door, I look behind him, hoping like hell that Hudson will be there with him... but he never is.

I haven't laid eyes on Hudson 'The Horror' Scott for a little over four weeks, but I've certainly heard enough to make it impossible to try and forget him.

Not that I ever could forget him anyway. I'm not sure who I think I'm kidding.

No matter how much I might want to, he's etched permanently into my brain, *and* my heart.

"Remind me again why he's taking this fight?" Juliet shoots me a sympathetic glance.

I don't know why she feels responsible for Justin's relentless whining, but she clearly does.

Truthfully, I'm not sure if he comes here to see me or her, he always gives me a hug, and then takes up his usual spot on the couch next to Jules.

That's when the moaning starts.

"Because he's an idiot." He drops his head into his hands and groans. "Sonny is a killer, even coming down a weight class; he's going to be brutal."

I shudder.

The last thing I want to hear about is someone 'brutal' being in a cage with the man I've fallen for but want to hate.

No matter what cruel things he said or did, I don't want anything bad to happen to him. I don't want to see him get hurt.

"So, he's going to get his ass kicked?" I ask nervously.

Justin glances up at me. "I honestly don't know – and that's what scares me."

"You never know who's going to win a fight, Justin," Juliet reminds him.

"But I *do*," he argues. "I haven't steered him wrong yet. He's undefeated in his professional career, and I'd really like to fucking keep it that way."

"Everyone loses sometimes," I mutter, and it's not until I say the words that I realise where I heard them.

It's exactly what Hudson told me when he walked me home that night – the night that changed everything between us.

"Not Horror," Justin argues and deep down, I agree.

Losing and Hudson don't go together in the same sentence.

He's a winner. He gets what he wants.

Me included.

Until he didn't want me anymore that is.

"How's the training going?" Juliet asks, steering Justin's focus back to her. "Is he looking good at least?"

"He's in the best shape of his life. He's put on a pound or two, but he's been grinding away in the gym so often it's been too hard to keep anything more on him."

I know that feeling. I've put on a pound or two myself. Given that I'm still drowning my sorrows in ice cream nearly every night, I guess it's to be expected.

"He's in there every day before I arrive, and if I don't physically force him to come with me when I go, he's still been training when I leave."

"Man on a mission, huh?" Juliet muses.

"I've never seen anything like it. Hudson has always been a hard bastard, but this is next level, even for him. It's like he's running from someone, or taking out his frustrations about something..." he turns his head to look at me. "Has he said anything to you?"

I shake my head. "Not a thing."

And it's the truth. Justin doesn't realise just how literally I mean that, but he seems satisfied with my answer. We haven't spoken a single word to one another.

Hudson's fight is tomorrow, and truthfully, I'm scared about what happens after – Justin is going to expect me to treat his injuries, and I don't know how the hell I'm going to manage to do that.

"You two are coming, right?" he asks then, as though the idea has only just occurred to him.

I feel the colour draining from my face and I couldn't pinpoint if it was down to the idea of seeing Hudson again, or the mere thought of the blood.

"I have to work late tomorrow night, so I'm out, sorry." Juliet shrugs.

I've never loved her more than I do right now.

I know damn well she doesn't have to work. She's giving me an out.

"I think I'll give it a miss after last time. I don't want to pass out and embarrass everyone again."

That's not a lie either – I'd only faint quicker if it was Hudson I had to hear getting hit.

Justin chuckles, and I'm glad he finds it amusing. "True." He flicks his gaze between me and Jules. "That sucks – I'll let you know how it goes."

I'll already know how it goes. I'll be watching it live – well, maybe not *watching*, but listening for the results.

"I'll get two tickets sent over just in case you finish early and Ram-Ram suddenly hardens up." He taps the end of Juliet's nose, and she grins at him.

I roll my eyes.

I'm going to have to talk to the pair of them.

They need to just get on with being together already. I'm sick of watching them dance around their feelings.

I've got enough of that going on in my own head.

"I'll see you girls later, I need to go make sure Horror hasn't snuck back into the gym."

I grab my laptop and snuggle down on the couch.

I wave out to Justin as Juliet walks him to the door, the pair of them giggling like school kids.

I narrow my eyes at their backs. He *definitely* comes here for her.

I bring up Google and type 'Hudson Scott vs Sonny Perez' into the search bar.

I don't know why I'm doing this to myself.

This is bound to bring up endless images of the sexy man with the eagle tattoo, but I need to see what he's up against.

I swallow the lump in my throat as I lay eyes on the man Hudson will be fighting in less than twenty-four hours.

His opponent is *huge* – shorter than Hudson the stats tell me, but built like a brick shit house.

Where Hudson is lithe and toned, this guy is bulky and sol-id.

They look nothing like a perfect match.

I wipe my palms on my leggings, I don't know why, but I feel ill all of a sudden.

I'm dying to pick up my phone and call Hudson so I can beg him not to go through with this fight, but it's all too late.

He'll fight, regardless of what I do or don't say – so I won't embarrass myself by trying.

"Are you okay?"

I tear my gaze from the screen and meet Juliet's eyes. She looks like she feels sorry for me.

I close my laptop quickly. I can't look at it any longer.

I shake my head. "I don't know what's wrong with me… it's been a month, I should be over him by now but instead I just feel sick to my stomach all the time."

"Should I get the ice cream?" she offers.

I shake my head again. "No, I seriously nearly puked this morning, I think I might have made myself intolerant to dairy or something."

She huffs out a laugh. "The amount you've been eating, I wouldn't be surprised."

She crosses the room and sits down in her spot on the other end of the couch. "You could just call him, you know?"

I fiddle with a loose string on the blanket I have draped across my lap. "I don't think that's a good idea. He's in the zone. He's got the fight to think about – he doesn't need me messing with his head."

"What about *your* head? That's the one I'm worried about."

I give her a grateful smile. "I'll be alright, I promise. I think I'm going to get an early night though – I'm super tired and I really don't feel so good."

The image of Hudson standing toe to toe with the man who looks like he could rip a car in half swirls though my mind.

It's enough to make anyone feel sick.

I feel her eyes on me as I leave the room, but I'm not in the mood for conversation.

I just want to crawl into bed and let sleep take me.

CHAPTER TWENTY-ONE

Hudson

"Go home, Horror, for fuck's sake, what are you still doing here?" Rusty demands.

I scowl at him. "What do you want?"

Justin must have sent him.

I'm one day out from the most important fight of my life, and I know I should be resting, but I can't sit still.

I can't get my brain to stop working and the only way I can figure out how to get my thoughts off her, is to run myself into the ground.

When I told her that everyone loses sometimes, I didn't know how right I was. Only it wasn't a fight that I lost; it was something far more important. It was her.

I can't sleep unless I'm physically exhausted, and if I can't sleep, I lie awake all night thinking about how the fuck I'm going to get Ramsey Ashton back, and *then* how I'll be willing to betray my best mate all over again if she'll have me.

It's a catch twenty-two. I want that girl more than anything, but I don't want to lose my best mate either.

I promised myself I'd give her space once I took this fight, mostly because she needed it – and I did too, but also because I've been working myself to the bone these past few weeks, so there's been no time for falling in love.

I've never, *ever* pushed myself this hard, but it was worth it – I feel more ready than ever.

And now that the fight is looming, my mind is shifting to what comes after.

Ramsey.

I hope to god this break has made her see things in the same clarity I have.

I might have been working my body to the bone, but inside I've been fighting my toughest battle yet – the one against my heart.

I fucked things up with her, but if there's even the tiniest of chances she'll take me back, then I'll do whatever it takes to make it happen – best mate be damned.

"Justin was worried you were going to get back on the bag," Rusty explains.

I huff out a breath. "Well you can tell the overreacting bastard that I'm strictly watching."

I turn away from Rusty and watch the young kid with the ginger hair – Oliver – working combos with one of the boxing trainers.

"He's looking good," Rusty observes.

"He certainly is."

"Might have to watch those belts, boy, there's a new fish in town."

I chuckle, but he's not wrong. Given another five years, Oliver could be where I was when my career started.

We watch in companionable silence for a few minutes.

"You seem different lately, man, what's going on with you?"

I glance at him out of the corner of my eye before going back to watching the fighters working their combos.

"I've got a lot on my mind."

"A girl with pink hair by any chance?" he questions.

I should deny it, but what's the point, he can clearly see more than I want him to, and I've been dying to talk to *someone* about this.

I glance at him again and there's no hint of taunting on his face.

"Maybe."

"She's as miserable as you are motivated," he mutters, shaking his head.

That's *not* what I want to hear. I don't need an ego feed – I need her happy.

If she's happy, I'll be happy.

"I don't know what's going on with you two, but you gotta make it right, Horror."

"I will. Trust me, man, I can't stand the distance between us – as soon as I'm done with this fight, I'll be knocking her door down. But I don't know what I'm gonna do about Justin."

He nods. "It's a tough spot, but I reckon it'll all work out." He claps me on the shoulder. "Unless you hurt her... then you're a dead man walking."

I'm all too aware.

I'm probably already a dead man walking if I'm honest.

"You ready?" he questions me.

I nod.

I don't know if he means to get out of here, or for the fight, or to get the girl back, but whichever it is, I'm as ready as I'll ever be.

CHAPTER TWENTY-TWO

Ramsey

"Why do you look like that?" Juliet frowns at me as I shuffle into the kitchen.

"I feel sick," I moan.

"You look like shit." She rakes her eyes over me, head to toe.

"Are you bleeding? I feel faint." I drop into a chair in a feeble attempt to settle my swirling head and gurgling stomach.

"There's no blood here."

"I feel like I'm—" I clutch my stomach. "I'm gonna—"

I rush to the sink and throw up noisily.

I feel Juliet come up behind me and turn the tap on to wash the stench away, and I feel her dabbing at my forehead with something cool.

"Oh god," I groan once I've emptied the contents of my stomach. "I'm swearing off ice cream for life, that last tub must have been bad."

She steers me around by the shoulders and sits me down in a chair.

"What's the time?" I ask as I wipe my mouth on the tissue she's offered me.

She glances at her cell. "Eleven. You slept *forever*."

I'm not surprised, I feel like shit.

"Why aren't you at work?"

"I had one clinic appointment today, so I got Sophie to cover it for me. I've been worried about you all morning."

"Don't tell Justin you've got the day off; he'll drag you to the fight tonight."

"Speaking of... the tickets arrived about nine." She points to the closed envelope on the table.

My stomach rolls again.

I'm not using those. No freaking way.

I glance up at Juliet and she's watching me closely.

"Get dressed and get in the car," she instructs suddenly.

"What, *why*? Where are we going?"

"To the doctor."

I wave her concerns off. "It's probably just food poisoning. I'll be fine."

"Nope." She shakes her head, letting out a deep sigh.

"What do you mean, nope? Why can't I have food poisoning?"

"Oh, you can, but I'm fairly sure you're pregnant."

My mouth drops open. "I'm sorry, *what*?"

"You know, *with child*."

"I know the definition of pregnant, Jules, for the love of god, I'm not an idiot, but I can't be knocked up... I just *can't* be... I'm only twenty-one."

"I'm pretty sure that's irrelevant," she says with a roll of her eyes and an impatient tap of her foot.

"But I can't be," I mutter to myself. "Why the hell do you think that?"

"You're nauseous, tired and I haven't seen any of those little plastic tampon wrapper thingys that you're not meant to flush floating in the toilet bowl for weeks now."

She's right. I missed my period and I've been too depressed to even notice.

"But we used a condom," I breathe, suddenly feeling a whole different type of sick.

"Two words – *fighter sperm*."

"That's not even funny." I groan.

"I wasn't kidding. *Look* at the guy – his sperm are bound to be bad-asses."

This *can't* be happening.

She's wrong. She has to be.

She works with animals, not people – she doesn't know what she's talking about.

"Only one way to find out," she says, as though she can read my thoughts.

"Shit."

She's right. And unfortunately for me, it involves me peeing on a stick.

***

"You know, I'm not sure you're meant to take that with you." She looks at the pee-covered stick that's sealed safely in a zip lock bag in disgust. "It's gross."

I don't know why I brought it with me.

The two pink lines are taunting me.

I'm hardly going to take it around to Hudson's house and hand it to him with a note saying 'congratulations soon-to-be daddy'.

Jesus Christ, what a mess.

I'm twenty-one years old, which isn't going to be the youngest mother in town, but it's still young enough, and to boot, I'm pregnant to my brother's best mate who happens to be a professional, scary-as-hell fighter.

"You're probably not wrong," I reply numbly as I stuff it into my bag.

I twist my charm bracelet around my wrist, pausing every time I get to the boxing glove charm he got for me. I guess I'll need a baby carriage one next.

We continue the drive in silence but I can tell she's dying to speak.

"What are you going to do?" she finally asks.

I shrug. "Just pretend it was food poisoning after all?" I offer weakly.

Truthfully, I have no idea what I'm going to do, other than the fact that I know I'm keeping it.

This baby is mine.

Whether or not its dad wants to be in the picture is another situation entirely.

Part of me wishes I'd never met Hudson Scott, but the rest of me couldn't be gladder.

I groan. I'm going to have to tell him, and sooner rather than later.

In fact, I wish I could just call him up and get it out of the way right now, but I'll never be able to reach him the day of his fight.

We talked about everything over those few weeks before we slept together, so I know his pre-fight routine like it was my own.

He barely talks to anyone the day of a fight.

He'll have his phone switched to flight mode so nothing comes in or out, and he'll have headphones on, blasting music to get him in the zone.

His circle is small, only Justin, Owen and Randy will be allowed access to the same room he's in.

He allows no press, no interviews, no fans.

This time is *his*.

"I'll tell him tomorrow," I murmur, to myself or Juliet, I'm not sure.

We pull up outside the house and I sigh.

It's the same house it was an hour ago, but everything is different now.

I didn't have the weight of the world on my shoulders then, like I do now.

I didn't have a list of midwifes and clinics clutched in my hand when I walked out that door, but I do now.

I may have had this tiny life growing inside of me then, but I didn't know about it like I do now.

I reach down and lay my hand across my stomach.

I can't believe I'm going to be a mother.

I'm only a few weeks along, they used a sensitive early detection kit, but there's no denying those two pink lines.

Juliet unlocks the front door, and I walk inside like I'm in a dream.

Nothing feels real.

I find myself in the kitchen, sitting at the table, but I don't even remember walking here.

I look down at my hands and I'm holding the envelope Justin had sent over.

I turn it over in my hands and slide my finger through the flap to open it.

I can hear Juliet rambling on about god only knows what, but my attention is solely on the envelope in my hands.

I open it and tug on the contents.

There are two tickets, as promised, but with it are two garlands with backstage access passes attached.

I glance up at Jules, but she's busy making me a cup of tea by the looks and talking about buying some decaf coffee when she goes to the store.

I look back to the items in my hand and my eye catches on a folded sheet of paper, tucked between the tickets.

I hold it in my shaky hands.

It's from him – I bet it is.

Justin isn't a note-writing kind of guy – no matter how deep he might be getting with my best friend.

It could be from Rusty or Beast, but it'd be likely to have a penis doodled on it if that were the case.

"Are you gonna open that, or just stare at it all afternoon?" Juliet demands, snapping me out of my daze.

She's sitting opposite me; my steaming cup of tea is on the table between us.

"What if it says he never wants to see me again?"

She snorts out a laugh. "Right, I bet that's what it says, along with tickets and VIP passes to his fight... because that seems like perfect logic."

"Alright, alright, know it all," I say with a roll of my eyes.

I flip the note open and my heart flutters at the sight of the scrawl of his writing.

I'm so screwed. Even his handwriting fills me with desire.

I swallow deeply and allow myself to read it.

Pinky,

I won't ask you to come, I'm bound to bleed and we all know how that goes, but I wanted you to know that I want you there.

Fuck I miss you.

We need to talk.

We need to do a lot of things.

I'll call you when this is done.

-H

We have *so* much to talk about. He literally has no idea just how much.

"Well?" Juliet asks impatiently.

"He wants me there," I whisper as I fold the note back in half, only to unfold it and read it all again.

He wants *me* there.

I don't know what to do with this information.

"Of *course* he does," Juliet remarks. "That man is in love with you, Ramsey. I don't know how you can't see that."

"I dunno, maybe it's the fact that I heard him with my own ears saying that falling in love with me was never going to happen, or maybe it was the sight of a girl he used to hook up with clutching his bare chest that did it for me," I reply, sarcasm thick in my tone.

She sighs. "I love you, girl, I really do, but I think you're being stupid. This isn't an easy situation to begin with – what if that was Justin he was talking to? What would you expect him to say? To confess he'd just come from your bed without even talking to you about it first?"

I shrug. She's making sense and it's making me feel like crap.

"And that bitch was a shit stirrer and you know it – even if they were together that night, which I doubt happened at all – you'd already pushed him away. It's not like he would have been cheating."

"So what am I meant to do?" I demand, my voice rising an octave. "You think I should go? Turn up to his fight and tell him that I'm in love with him?"

I slam my palm down on the table top in frustration.

Juliet grins widely. "About time you admitted that out loud."

I groan and rest my forehead against the table. "You win... I'm in love with him. I love him and it's all messed up and Justin is going to flip, and now there's a baby and what the fuck am I going to do?"

"You're going to get dressed into something killer, and then we're going to watch a fight."

I groan again.

I had a feeling that's what she was going to say.

CHAPTER TWENTY-THREE

Hudson

The intricate melody washes over me, my pulse thrumming in time to the heavy beat.

My eyes are closed, my brain running through the combos over and over again.

There's an hour until go time.

I picture my opponent in my mind. I imagine him falling to the canvas, landing like the heavy sack of shit he's bound to be.

I don't have the advantage out there today, not weight wise anyway.

He could have put on more than five pounds overnight after our weigh in.

The dude is massive.

But I'm fast, strong and lean.

I'm not going to bow down and be the easy beat he's expecting, that's for damn sure.

I feel someone nudge my shoulder and I open my eyes.

Justin, Randy and Owen are all standing around me.

Gang's all here.

I tug the headphones from my ears and hit pause on my playlist.

I hand them to Owen, and he sits them down on the table opposite me.

"Let's get those hands wrapped and then we'll get you warmed up."

I nod.

Justin drags a chair over and sits directly in front of me, a pair of hand wraps in his hands.

I'm sitting backwards in my chair, my wrists resting on the highest point of the chair so he has easy access.

He begins with my left hand, wrapping the fabric down my wrist and then back up again before wrapping it around my palm. My thumb is next and then my fingers.

The only thing between the skin on my knuckles and my opponent's body is these thin layers of fabric and my four-ounce MMA gloves.

It's nothing, but it's a hell of a lot more than the rest of my body gets.

"You feeling good?" Justin asks, his eyes trained on what he's doing to my hands.

"I feel ready." I nod.

He doesn't reply. He's knows I'm not much of a talker when I'm prepping for a fight.

I have no fucking idea if I'll come out of this thing on top, but I'll give it my best shot, that much I know for certain.

I've trained harder for this than I ever have for anything in my life.

He finishes with my left hand and I lift my right.

He repeats the action all over again as Owen starts kneading at my shoulders.

They're tight, tensed and ready to go.

I've never been quite this strong or powerful.

Sonny is going to be in for a surprise.

I bounce my knee, my favourite pair of MMA shorts sliding up and down my thigh.

The nerves are kicking in and I welcome them. It's all part of my process.

I hear someone stumble and I look up to the door with a scowl.

Whoever it is should know better than to be in here right now, but when my eyes land on her pink hair, shock replaces my irritation.

I'm so stunned by the sight of her beautiful face and sexy body that I can't speak.

"Ramsey?" Justin says quickly, flying to his feet. "What are you doing back here?"

Her eyes widen as she looks between me and her brother, her cheeks blushing scarlet.

"I'm so sorry, I shouldn't have come in. I'll see you guys later."

She turns and rushes from the doorway, and I'm out of my seat and following her before I even think about it.

Justin reaches out and catches my arm. "We need to get you warmed up."

I shrug him off and carry on towards the door. "I just want five minutes to see if she's okay."

I don't look back over my shoulder to see his reaction, because frankly, I don't care what he thinks about me chasing Ramsey.

Like taking this fight, it's just something I *have* to do.

I don't hear anyone following me, and I'm fucking grateful for that; I'm not exactly in the mood for minding my words.

"Ramsey," I call after her retreating frame, my voice a hoarse growl.

She turns and looks at me over her shoulder, her expression mortified, but she doesn't stop.

She spins back around, already moving faster and crashes straight into one of the servers from the bar.

"Fuck," I grunt, as she falls to the ground, her bag contents spilling all over the hallway.

I jog to her and reach for her elbow to help her sit up.

"I'm so sorry," the server apologises profusely.

"It's okay," Ramsey says at the same time I say, "Just go."

He takes one look at me and scarpers back to wherever he came from.

"Pinky," I breathe as she looks up at me, her golden eyes still wide as saucers. "You came."

She drops her gaze and starts reaching around for the contents of her bag. "I'm sorry, I should have known you were busy, I just wanted to tell you that I was here... that I got your note..." she mutters as she stuffs lipsticks, pens and all kinds of other shit back into her huge bag.

I can feel my heart thumping in my chest.

This isn't what I need right now, but I can't walk away from her again, not like this.

I start picking things up and passing them to her.

I hear her gasp and I glance down at the thing being passed between her hand and mine.

My heart rate increases.

It's a pregnancy test. A positive one.

"Is that..."

"Hudson," she says, her voice no more than a whisper.

"Is that…" I try again, but still fail. "Are you…"

She scrambles to her feet, tugging the positive pregnancy test from my hand.

"You're pregnant?" I demand as I stand.

She looks up at me, tears pooling in her eyes and nods. "I only found out today," she whispers.

"Is it mine?"

She drops her gaze, but I'm not having it, I grip her chin and force her eyes back to mine.

"Is. That. Baby. Mine?"

She nods again, and I feel myself release a breath. I don't know if I'm more shocked or relieved.

I'm going to be a *father* but given that she's going to be our baby's mother, the idea doesn't seem to be knocking me the way it should be.

"I'm sorry," she says again, and the tone in her voice almost breaks my heart. "We didn't mean for this to happen… we used protection…"

"Ramsey."

"I don't know how it happened…" she continues. "If you don't want any part of it, I totally understand."

"You didn't just say that," I growl, my eyes narrowing.

A lone tear slides down her cheek and the need to make it go away threatens to overwhelm me.

"I won't force you to do something you're not ready for, you can have as little or as much involvement as you want… god I'm *so* sorry."

I've really done a number on this woman.

Here she is, standing in front of me, telling me I'm about to become a father, and she's *scared*, terrified even of the fact that I might not want anything to do with her *or* my baby.

She couldn't be more wrong.

I wasn't planning on becoming a dad, not yet, and I certainly wasn't planning on getting her pregnant when we weren't even officially together, but that's what's happened.

Life might give me hell at times, but I always push back twice as hard, and this will be no exception.

I'm a fighter, it's what I do... and I'll fight for her. I'll fight harder for her than I've fought for anything else.

Her *and* my child.

I release her chin and step closer towards her, my hands that are wrapped tightly, ready to inflict pain, sliding around her middle in the softest of touches.

I tug her into my chest, and she falls against me, her arms snaking tightly around my neck and clinging on for dear life.

"You have nothing to be sorry for," I whisper into her ear as I slowly and gently rub my hand up and down her back. "We didn't plan this, but there's always that risk."

She nods, snivelling.

"We're in this together, pinky."

She looks up at me, her lashes holding evidence of her pain. "We're *not* together though."

"And that's my fault. I fucked up."

"Hudson, you don't need to say anything," she says, her voice pleading with me. "I shouldn't even be here, you have a fight soon and I'm messing with your head... I—"

I can't fucking take it anymore.

She thinks I don't want her.

I'll fucking show her.

I drop my lips to hers and kiss her into silence.

She pulls back in surprise, my name falling from her lips before she leans back in and welds our mouths together again.

This is so reckless, claiming her out here where anyone could see, but I'm past caring.

She's mine.

I'm hers.

It's about time the rest of the world caught up.

I hear the booming voice over the loud speaker in the main arena, announcing that there is forty minutes until the start of the fight.

"Shit," I murmur as I pull away from her.

Her eyes slowly open, her teeth sinking into her bottom lip.

I grin, my heart swelling. She's so fucking perfect, and she's all mine.

"I've gotta go."

She nods, but her grip on me tightens. She pushes up to her tip toes and brushes her lips against mine once more before letting go.

"We'll talk after?" I question, unwilling to walk away even though I know I'm out of time.

She nods.

I still don't move.

"Go," she demands, shoving me in the direction of my changing room.

I chuckle and head in that direction.

I get only about four steps away when I stop and turn back to her.

She's still standing right where I left her, watching me, one of her hands resting on her still-flat stomach.

It hits me again then. I'm going to be a dad.

I can't help the grin that spreads across my face.

"You're going to be late," she warns me.

I shrug.

She rolls her eyes. "We'll talk after."

"I know." I nod, still unmoving.

She pops a brow in question.

There's something I need to say now, something I need off my chest before I go out there under the spotlight.

"You asked me a question – I know you were just repeating the horrible shit you heard me say, but I still wanted to give you an answer."

"What are you talking about?" She frowns.

"You asked me what I thought was going to happen with us, if I thought we were going to fall in love and run off into the sunset."

Recognition dawns and I swear she looks like she's going to cry again.

"I don't know about the sunset part, Ramsey, but the rest of it – that's *exactly* what I thought was going to happen. From the moment I saw you, I wanted forever."

"Hudson," she breathes as I turn away and head back to my team.

"I love you, Ramsey Ashton," I call out to her, over my shoulder. "Always have, always will."

She doesn't answer, but when I reach the doorway I can't help but look back at her.

"Hey, champ," she calls after me, "good luck."

I smirk. I've got all the luck I need right here.
I've got her.

CHAPTER TWENTY-FOUR

Ramsey

I float back to my seat in a daze.

He knows I'm pregnant and he didn't yell, or get angry, or try to blame me for doing it on purpose or anything crazy like that.

I'd *never* do that, but in the world he lives in, one of fame and fortune – it's not entirely uncommon for women to give it a shot.

I lower myself to the chair, all too aware of Juliet's eyes on me and trail my fingers over my swollen lips longingly.

I can still *feel* where he kissed me, his mouth hot and firm.

I've never seen a person in the shape he's in tonight; even his lips were rock hard.

He's a wall of pure muscle and strength, and I almost pity the man brave enough to take him on – *almost*.

"Oh my god, spill already," Juliet demands, grabbing my arm and shaking it.

I snap out of my day dream, look at her with a stupid, sappy grin... and tell her *every* little detail.

"Be still my beating heart." She swoons when I'm done, clutching her chest for dramatic effect. "He *really* said all that?"

I nod and nibble on my lip. I honestly can't believe it either.

Obviously, there's still so much we need to talk about and iron out, but as long as he loves me, and I love him, which I *re-*

ally fucking do – then we can make it through the rest. I know we can.

But first he has to make it out of that cage unscathed.

"Where do I find myself a sexy fighter boy who's going to whisper sweet nothings in my ear?" Juliet gushes.

I pin her with my stare. "I think we both already know the answer to that."

She blushes.

"You should tell him how you feel – as disgusting as it might be." I mock shudder.

She rolls her eyes at me. "Check you, miss thang, you finally go get your man and now you think you can just go dishing out advice?"

I burst into laughter and she joins me.

I don't know what I would have done without my best friend these past few weeks, *today* especially. She's been my rock.

I would have been even more of a hot mess than I already am.

"Are you nervous?" she asks me, her eyes drifting to the cage and the thousands of people in the huge arena surrounding it.

"Honestly, I'm freaking out," I admit.

We're only a few rows back, and I'm starting to feel sick about it all over again.

I had good intentions coming tonight, but the reality is, that if I sit here, I'm going to see things I don't want to see and hear things I don't want to hear.

I have faith in Hudson's ability to win this fight, but I'm not an idiot. There will be blood and there will definitely be pain.

Nobody steps into that cage and comes out completely unscathed – not even my champ.

"I'd be freaking out if my baby daddy was about to take on *that* as well." She grimaces as she points to the photo of Sonny on the brochure in her hand.

"Shhhh," I hiss at her, before glancing around to make sure no one heard.

The last thing I need is the media getting hold of that little snippet of information.

Hudson might have a reputation that keeps him from being hounded by his fans in public, but the press won't afford him the same luxury – not with a story like that.

"Shit, *sorry*." She winces. "I'm not very good with secrets."

I roll my eyes at her. "Well, you've managed not to let it slip that you're in love with my brother or that I'm in love with his best friend, so I think you're doing better than you give yourself credit for."

She opens her mouth to argue, but she's cut off by the dimming of the lights and the announcer's voice booming over the sound system.

I take a deep breath in an attempt to settle my racing heart, but it's no use, there's no calming me down now.

I don't hear a word the announcer says, but even I can't miss the thud of the heavy beat and the applause of the crowd as Sonny Perez enters the arena, a black robe covering his body. He steps into the cage and shrugs it off.

I gasp.

He's even bigger than I imagined.

Hell, he's bigger than big... the dude is *huge* and terrifying looking.

"Oh my god," Juliet whispers, clutching my arm as we look on in terror.

It's lucky she's holding on to me right now; it's the only thing stopping me from flying out of my seat and running back to where I left Hudson so I can beg him not to go through with this.

Sonny punches the air, his huge arms tensing.

"This is *not* good," I whisper.

"This is a fucking disaster, what the hell was he thinking taking a fight against this ape? Does he want to lose his belt or something?"

"Who gives a fuck about the *belt*?" I hiss, "I'm more concerned about his neck getting snapped."

Jesus.

I need to calm down.

I shouldn't be underestimating Hudson like this, but *shit*, this guy is massive.

I try again to steady my breathing, and when I hear the announcer say the words 'Hudson 'The Horror' Scott', it almost works.

His walkout song begins to play, and I instantly feel at ease as I recognise the beat of Phil Collins, *In The Air Tonight*.

I must have heard this song a dozen times over the time we spent together, either blaring over the sound system or through the earbuds we shared sitting side by side.

The airy melody floats through the air, turning the head of every person in the place.

The tunnel he'll emerge from remains dark, but he's there – I can feel it.

He'll be jogging on the spot, his left hand with a slight nervous twitch.

The beat drops and red spotlights flash to the man with the black and white shorts.

His torso is bare and exposed, and it makes my belly flip.

He jogs forward, and the crowd goes wild.

I know Justin will be behind him somewhere with Randy and Owen, two of them are bound to be holding Hudson's belts high above their heads – he's the champ here after all, but I don't even see them.

All I see is Hudson as he struts – there really is no other way to explain that confidence-filled walk – closer and closer to the cage.

He's going to walk right by us.

Juliet's grip tightens on my arm, and I grip her back just as firmly.

Hudson approaches us, and I wait for him to pass by and enter the cage.

I glance back into the cage, looking for his opponent, so when I hear Hudson's voice, I jump in surprise.

"Make sure you close your eyes, pinky," he growls, pausing only briefly as he brushes past.

My mouth drops open, and he grins wickedly.

He turns back to the cage and just like that, he's back in the zone.

I watch with shaking hands as he strolls in, as though this isn't one of the biggest fights in his life.

The two men circle each other like sharks, sizing each other up, and while Sonny still looks just as threatening, I have to admit that I feel better now that Hudson is in front of him.

My man is *strong*, there's not an ounce of fat on his frame – he's literally built for this.

If anyone is going to take Sonny down, it's Hudson.

He turns to the crowd, and the terrifying glint in his dark eyes gives me goose bumps.

"I take back my previous statement," Juliet whispers. "I don't care how big that other dude is – Hudson is going to *kill* him."

I nod in agreement as the referee drags the two men into the centre of the cage.

He barks his orders at them and gestures for them to touch gloves.

Hudson holds out his hand, but Sonny turns his back – refusing to complete the sportsmanly gesture.

Hudson smirks, and that's when I know it for certain – he'll win this fight if it kills him.

"You ready for this?" Juliet asks me.

My stomach lurches and I shake my head. "Not even a little bit."

The ding sounds, indicating the start of the first round and I know I shouldn't look, but I can't seem to pull my eyes away.

Hudson prowls, like an agile cat towards its prey.

The two men dance around each other for a few seconds, and when Sonny charges like a raging bull, Hudson is ready, faster, sharper and more accurate.

He shifts, ever so subtly to the left, and the big man misses.

Hudson shifts again and swings his leg, fast as lightening. The crack as it hits Sonny's jaw rings in my ears.

I squeeze my eyes shut. "I think I've seen enough," I whisper.

"Shut your eyes," Juliet instructs, and I feel her pulling forward – she's literally on the edge of her seat as I hear the two men exchanging blows and the crowd cheering and screaming.

I shake off her hand and cover my ears.

I'm starting to feel dizzy.

I'm considering making a run for it when a firm hand grips my shoulder.

I risk a glance and see Rusty smiling down at me. "You alright there, babe?" he asks, his tone amused.

I shake my head. "Nope."

He chuckles. "He told me you'd need an out."

I frown at him.

"Well, come on." He holds out his hand to me. "I'm your out."

I take his hand gratefully without so much as a backwards glance at my violence-loving best friend as he leads me away from the cage and out of the main arena, into the back.

Juliet will have to manage on her own. That girl has turned feral.

My brother is messing with her head.

"He told me to get you to wait back here," Rusty instructs as I fall gratefully onto a couch in the corner. "He said you'd probably want to watch the fight on the TV – on mute?" He frowns at me like he thinks I'm crazy, but I don't care, I'm too busy swooning over the fact that Hudson knows exactly what I need.

"Don't judge me," I say with a grin. "I can watch with no noise or listen with no pictures – not both."

He hits a few buttons on the remote and the TV in front of me flickers to life, the volume muted.

It's the end of round one, Justin and Owen are in the cage with Hudson. Justin is talking at him – not to him – *at* him and Owen is icing his shoulder blades.

There's no blood on his face yet and I'm grateful for it.

Even through a TV screen it still makes me feel woozy.

"You want me to sit with you?" Rusty asks, as he lingers in the doorway – clearly dying to get back out amongst the action.

I snort out a laugh. "I could say yes, and you'd have to stay, am I right?"

I don't know how much Rusty knows about Hudson and me, but it's clear he's been given his orders.

He shakes his head and smirks. "No comment."

"Go." I wave him away. "I'm fine here. Just keep an eye on Juliet, would you? I think she's starting to go a bit savage."

He laughs loudly, throwing his head back. "You need to join us on the dark side, Ramsey, it's fun, I promise."

I roll my eyes and glance back at the screen to see the referee ushering both men back into the centre.

Nerves settle in my belly again and I tuck my legs under my body.

"I'll see you after," Rusty calls, "Try not to puke!"

I flip the middle finger at his retreating frame and then he's gone.

"C'mon, champ," I mutter as the second round begins. "You can do this."

CHAPTER TWENTY-FIVE

Hudson

This fight has been brutal.

I've never been hit so hard in my life. I'm more than holding my own, but he just won't go down, and I need him to go down – preferably two rounds ago.

"Alright, bro, this is it – last round. If you're going to win this thing by knockout, now is your time."

I nod my head and blink as blood dribbles down my face.

I've split that fucking eye brow again.

Owen grabs a towel and wipes the blood away before smearing more Vaseline on it to try and control the bleeding.

It's not likely to help much.

I hope Ramsey isn't watching.

I know I shouldn't be thinking about her right now, but that's not going to stop me.

She's here and she's going to be mine.

Not only that, but she's going to make me a dad.

I feel the corner of my mouth twitch with a grin.

"Are you listening to me?" Justin demands, snapping me from my fantasy and back to reality.

"I'm listening."

"Get deep into that head, man, and find the thing that means the most to you."

He looks at me pointedly and I nod, picturing Ramsey.

"Now get to your god damn feet and finish this fight – do it for whatever is in your head right now."

I nod again, this time really hearing his words.

I'll do this. For Ramsey, and my baby.

For my family.

The word family circles through my mind and suddenly I feel invincible.

I don't feel tired, or sore, or beaten.

I feel like I've been shocked back to life.

This is mine.

"He's tired. He's hurt." Justin grips me on the shoulders and looks me dead in the eye. "*Finish him.*"

Owen pushes my mouth guard back into my mouth, and I snarl.

I stalk to the centre of the canvas and stare hard at the man who dared to take me on. The man who stepped into the cage bigger and stronger than me. The man who I'm about to beat.

No one is taking that belt home but me.

The ref drops his hand and I feel myself flying across the distance. I've let him come to me – make the first moves all fight, but the time for that is over.

My shin connects with his jaw and his head snaps back.

That one was for Ramsey.

I give him no time to recover before I'm on him again, my fists flying in a flurry of combos.

I hear Justin screaming something, but I can't make sense of it.

Sonny shoves back, his guard falling, and I swing, catching him clean across the nose.

That one was for my baby.

He pushes forward, his arms wrapping around my neck in a grapple, but it's weak – he's losing – I shove him off and his hands come high to guard his face.

I drop my right elbow and swing with every last bit of strength I can find, forcing my fist into the underside of his chin with an uppercut.

He falls to the canvas, out like a light.

I breathe heavily as I stand over him, my shoulders rising and falling.

That one was for my family.

The crowd goes wild, screaming and chanting my name as the ref dives between us waving his hands back and forth, signalling that the fight is over.

I *won*.

I stagger backwards, the weight of my achievement overwhelming me.

I won.

I actually fucking did it.

I close my eyes and absorb the moment.

I did it. For me, for her, for us.

Justin, Owen and Randy are in the ring when I open my eyes again and heaving my belts onto my shoulders, one on each side.

I spin around the cage, my disorientated eyes searching the crowd, even though I know she never would have been able to stomach watching that.

I want to see her.

The fight is over now and all I care about is finding my girl and making things right between us.

I get passed from person to person around the cage, getting hugged, clapped on the back and congratulated.

I have what feels like endless mics and cameras stuck in my face; everyone wants a piece of the action.

The crowd is cheering and yelling and all of a sudden, I've just had enough.

"Let's roll." Justin throws his hand up in the air and circles it, gesturing to my team to round up and get out.

He knows me well. That fact is only going to make it even harder to break it to him about me and Ramsey.

We shuffle out of the cage, security guards clearing a path for me to escape.

I see Justin collect Juliet on the way past and I grin.

Maybe he'll understand after all, he's like a moth to a flame with that girl.

Randy jogs ahead – my ice bath will be waiting, but unlike usual, I don't want to spend hours resting.

I just want to see her.

She's the only treatment I need.

"I just have to do something," I tell the guys as I lag behind.

Justin frowns at me. "What the fuck could you possibly need to do right now?"

"I'll be there in a minute, just give me a sec to myself." I tip my head in the direction of my change room, gesturing for them to go on ahead of me.

His frown deepens but he does as I've asked, leading Juliet into the change room with him, Owen following.

I wait for them to disappear and then cross the hall, heading for the room I know Ramsey will be waiting for me in.

I can't count on Rusty for much these days, but I knew he'd take care of her for me.

I knock lightly on the door and I hear her sweet voice call out, "Come in."

I push the door open and it's not until her eyes land on me that everything hits me.

Her, me, our baby, my fight.

"Oh my god." She makes a gagging sound, and I rush forward, reaching her just in time for her to throw up into the rubbish bin next to the couch.

"Ramsey, are you okay?"

"It's the—" she gags again. "It's the b—"

"The baby?" I interrupt her, "Ramsay, is something wrong with the baby?" I demand.

A deathly cold voice comes from behind me.

"It's the *blood*."

Fuck. The blood.

Fuck. The voice.

I jump away from her and in the same action, turn to meet the man I know is behind me.

Justin is seething, his chest heaving up and down as he glares at me. "Tell me you *didn't* knock up my baby sister."

I take a slow, calculated step in his direction. "I can't tell you that."

He winces like I've smacked him clean across the face.

"You're dead."

"*Justin*," Ramsey whispers from behind me. "Don't."

"Outside," I demand, pointing at the door. "We're not doing this in front of her."

"Agreed," Justin grunts, his face twitching with the physical restraint he's exerting to stop himself from mauling me here and now.

He turns and stalks out the door, and I move to follow.

"Hudson, please don't," she begs me.

I don't turn. I can't. One look at my face and she'll faint or throw up again.

"No matter what happens, stay here until I come back for you, you understand?"

"Hudson," she whimpers.

"It's going to be okay, pinky, I promise. I should have done this a long time ago."

I stride from the room and I hear her start to cry.

It breaks my fucking heart to leave her like that, but I have to do this.

We have to get this out in the open if there's ever going to be a chance for us to stay in each other's lives.

He's my best mate. He's going to be my kid's uncle.

He pushes forward when he sees me close the door behind me, and swings wide, missing me by a mile.

"Justin, just fucking listen," I say as I dodge another swing.

"*Listen*? To *what*?" he demands. "How you went behind my back and fucked my sister and got her pregnant? Is *that* what you want me to listen to?"

"It's not like that."

He charges at me, and I slip to the side.

We're circling each other like we're in the cage, only difference is there's no referee here – there's no one to stop us from killing one another.

"What's it like then, Horror?" he yells at me, his voice rising.

"I love her. I want to be with her for the rest of my fucking life!" I yell back.

His step falters and his hands fall to his sides.

The dance stops.

We're standing opposite one another, neither of us moving.

"You *love* her?"

I nod. "Haven't you ever just met someone and felt something you knew you shouldn't for them right away?" I ask, already knowing full well that his answer will be yes. He has – hell, he still is.

"Fuck yes, I have," he thunders, his arms visibly shaking.

"So, what did you do about it?"

"Buried that shit down deep." He sneers. "Tucked it away under jokes and teasing and tried to forget it ever existed."

"And how's that fucking working for you?" I demand, my own breathing becoming laboured.

"It's *not*," he admits with a growl. "But that's the way it has to be."

"That's bullshit and you know it."

This time when he charges at me, I let him make contact, and he takes us both to the ground with a loud thud.

He lays into my already battered and bruised face, and I have to admit, the bastard has still got a mean right cross.

I don't even hit him back – I've got no right. He deserves to be angry.

"What the fuck?" I hear Rusty's voice and feel Justin being lifted off me.

I swipe at the blood pouring from my nose and see Beast holding Justin back as he struggles to get free.

"He knocked up my sister," Justin growls.

Beast glances at me. "Shit, Horror, for real?"

I nod and Justin struggles harder.

"Calm the fuck down," he demands.

Justin stills.

Rusty holds his hand out to help me, and I drag my ass up.

Justin points his finger at me. "You *knew* what this would do to us, and you went and did it anyway."

My heart is racing but there's no fight left in me. I don't want to fight him – I just want him to understand.

I want him to accept us.

"I know I did," I agree.

"So you made your choice. You chose her."

"I did."

He goes to speak again, but I cut him off.

"I'm not going to stand here and apologise for it. I chose her. I'd choose her again, over everyone and anyone. Even you."

I see him balk, but I can't stop now.

"I know that makes me a shitty mate, but it is what it is. Ramsey deserves someone who will put her before everything else, and I intend to do exactly that for the rest of my life, if she'll let me."

I can see the war he has going on in his head.

"Do you really think she deserves anything less?" I demand.

"No, but—"

"No buts. You know I'll look after her better than anyone else ever could. I'll never let anything happen to her, or to our child, you have my word. I'll put her above *everything*. Even if it costs me our friendship, I still choose her."

He looks at me with hollow eyes.

"Let me go," he hisses at Beast.

He reluctantly lets him go, and Justin shrugs him off.

"I'm out of here," he says, and he turns and leaves.

Rusty blows out a deep breath as he watches him go. "Well fuck."

Can't argue with that.

"Let's get you cleaned up, man."

"I need to see Ramsey," I argue.

"Not looking like that you don't," he points out.

I touch the blood dripping down my face.

Fuck. He's right.

He shoves me in the direction of my changing room.

"I'll get Juliet to go and see her," he reassures me.

I nod in acceptance.

It's the only choice I've got.

CHAPTER TWENTY-SIX

Ramsey

He bursts through the door, his hair still wet from his shower – but his cuts stitched and covered, thankfully.

I wipe at the tears under my eyes.

"Pinky," he breathes, hurt in his tone as he drops to his knees in front of me.

"I'll give you two a minute," Juliet says as she rises from the spot next to me and disappears out the door, closing it softly behind her.

"He didn't take it well."

"I know," I say as I reach out to run my fingers carefully through his hair.

He's got bruises along his cheekbone and jaw, and swelling to his brow where it's been cut open yet again. His lip is split, but it's only small.

"You heard?" he questions.

I nod.

I heard every word, every scuffle, every punch.

"You really love me that much?" I whisper.

His dark eyes, intense with worry, soften as he reaches for me. "I love you that much and more, I promise I'll never be so stupid again, I'll never hurt you."

He wraps his strong arms around my waist and tucks his face into my shirt.

This is the most vulnerable I've ever seen him.

He's begging me – for forgiveness – for another chance.

It blows my mind that I have the power to bring Hudson Scott to his knees.

"It's not all your fault… I jumped to conclusions; I should have just talked to you."

He pulls back a fraction and looks up at me, his expression serious. "I need you to know that nothing was going on with me and Vanessa. She shouldn't have even been there, but I'm sorry that she was. I threw her out when you left – she won't be back."

"You don't need to explain."

"I *want* to."

I stroke my fingers over his scalp again.

"I know you heard me on the phone that morning."

I nod, biting my lip nervously.

"I didn't mean what I said."

"I know," I whisper. "I'm sorry I thought the worst."

I should have asked him about it. I shouldn't have just assumed.

"Justin was hounding me about spending time with you and I needed him off my case; he was ruining the best night I'd ever had."

My mouth curves up into a grin. "The best night you ever had?"

"Fuck yes," he growls, his hands tentatively coming around to my stomach and rubbing it gently. "I can't believe we're having a baby."

"Neither can I," I admit.

"I'm going to love that kid as much as I love you, pinky."

Tears well in my eyes again, only this time for totally different reasons.

"Hudson, there's something I need to tell you," I whisper.

He freezes, his eyes coming up to meet mine.

"I love you, champ."

He grins, wider than I've ever seen him smile.

"That's good, baby, that's *real* good."

***

"I'll get it," I call out to Hudson as I rush towards the front door.

I squeeze past the stack of boxes in the hallway and nearly trip on a bag of clothes as I stumble towards the front door.

I catch myself and tug the door open.

"Justin," I breathe as my eyes land on the man on the other side.

He's about the last person I expected to see here.

Neither Hudson nor I have heard from him in a month.

"Hey, Ram-Ram," he mutters, his tone guilty.

"You're here."

He nods, his head dipping to avoid my gaze.

"You're here," I repeat, my tone moving from shocked to relieved. "Holy shit I missed you," I cry as I throw myself into his arms.

He stumbles back but manages to catch me, his deep chuckle at my ear.

"I missed you, too," he replies as he hugs me tightly.

I hold him for far longer than is in any way necessary, but I'm scared to let go. I'm not sure I can go another month without seeing my brother again.

He loosens his hold and glances behind me.

"Juliet told me you were moving in here."

I raise a brow at him. "Oh, I see how it is, Juliet first, your own sister second."

He has the good sense to look embarrassed at least.

"You tell that girl how you feel this time?" I ask.

He nods. "Took a leaf out of someone else's book and put my feelings first."

I smile at him, butterflies fluttering in my stomach. "About time."

He grins, and I don't think I've ever seen him look so happy.

"So, what happened?"

"Turns out she loves me back."

"No shit." Hudson's voice comes from behind me.

He stops in the doorway and leans against the frame, his arm snaking out to wrap around my middle, his hand splayed protectively across my belly.

The two men stare hard at one another for what feels like an eternity, neither one backing down from their hard stare.

Justin is the first to cave, a smile pulling at the corners of his lips. It doesn't take long before they're both grinning at each other like idiots.

"Does this mean you two are making up?" I ask hopefully.

"If he'll forgive me for being a hot head?" Justin asks with a grimace.

"If he'll forgive me for knocking up his sister?" Hudson counters.

I smack his chest playfully. "Oh, that's *real* nice."

"It's all water under the bridge as far as I'm concerned." Justin nods, his eyes searching Hudson's face for a clue that they're okay.

Hudson steps forward, one arm still around me, and extends his other hand to Justin. "It's forgotten."

Justin takes his hand, but instead of shaking it, pulls him in for a hug.

Tears well in my eyes as I get half dragged into their reunion moment.

"Are you *crying*?" Justin asks as he steps back.

I scowl at him and wipe at the stray drops of moisture. "I'm pregnant, you asshole – I have a lot of hormones. And my boyfriend and my brother just made up, and you and Juliet are finally together, and I'm just so happy," I sob.

"Jesus," Justin drawls. "Good luck with that, man."

Hudson tucks me in closer to him and kisses the top of my head. "Ignore him, pinky, he's just not man enough to deal with feelings."

Both men chuckle.

"Why are you covered in paint?" Justin asks suddenly, as though he's only just noticed that Hudson has splatters of paint on him from head to toe.

"I'm painting the nursery." He grins, and my ovaries just about explode.

He's the most caring, sweet and considerate father already.

"You better have picked a good colour for my niece or nephew," Justin says as he pushes past Hudson and into the house.

"Hey! Don't touch anything in there, you'll fuck it up," Hudson calls after him as Justin heads upstairs.

Hudson kisses my head again and takes off after his best mate. "I mean it, Justin, keep your mitts off my kid's room."

I sigh and smile to myself.

Just like old times.

EPILOGUE

Hudson

"You want me to take her, baby?" I ask, my voice a whisper as I find my beautiful girls hiding away in a quiet corner.

Ramsey shakes her head at me, a soft smile on her lips. "She's out to it. I'll come back out in a minute."

I lean in, my intention to brush my lips against hers, but she deepens the kiss, gripping my shirt in her fist as she tugs me closer.

She bites down on my bottom lip and sucks it into her mouth.

My dick jumps.

I'm dying to be inside my girlfriend again. It's been a long time.

"*Jesus*, Ramsey," I growl.

"Guess what today is?" she asks, her forehead resting against mine, our daughter cradled between us.

"Opening day?" I guess.

"Not just opening day, champ, although I guess that's as fitting of a term as any..."

I frown, and she giggles softly.

"It's been six weeks since Sienna was born," she replies, her voice implying she's got more to tell me. "The doctor gave me the all clear. I guess the doors to the gym won't be the only thing opening tonight."

Jesus.

"Is it time to leave?" I groan. "I think I'm ready to go."

She giggles again and shoves my chest lightly. "You can't ditch your own opening night."

I don't care what she says. I couldn't care less about cutting a ribbon or schmoozing the sponsors.

There is one thing and one thing only on my mind right now.

She must be doing a fine job of reading my mind because she laughs and rolls her eyes.

"Go," she insists. "I'm not going anywhere; we've got all the time in the world."

We sure fucking do.

But I still haven't moved.

"Hudson, go." She giggles, shooing me in the direction of our guests.

I chuckle and do as I'm told.

If someone had told me a year ago that I'd be here, opening my own gym for the purpose of training underprivileged kids and keeping them out of trouble, I'd have said they were insane. I guess if someone had have told me that I would have a baby with my best friend's little sister, I would have laughed too. But all that changed with just one look.

"Horror!" Justin bellows across the room. "Photos!" I wave at him in acknowledgement and head over, shaking hands and exchanging pleasantries with our guests as I go.

Justin tugs me to his side, and we pose for half a dozen photos.

Justin, Ramsey and I are business partners in the gym – Justin and I coach, and Ramsey will run her physiotherapy clinic from here whenever she's ready to work again.

"Over here, boys." One of the photographers clicks his fingers at us and we look in his direction.

"Better work on that grin before the big shoot," he taunts me.

I flip him off. "Fuck off, Ryan, I won't be smiling, trust me on that."

"What's this?" Justin asks excitedly.

I groan. I'd done so well at keeping this from him.

Once that loud mouth finds out, the whole world will know.

"The champ here has agreed to do a photoshoot for a sexy calendar," the photographer tells him, and I groan.

"A fucking *what*?" Justin demands, his grin widening. "You're joking?"

I shake my head in disbelief.

"Oh, this is too good." He howls with laughter. "Like nude?"

"No, not fucking nude," I growl.

He looks at me expectantly.

"*Shirtless*." I grind out the word.

He laughs even harder. "I can't believe this. Wait until I tell the guys."

"Justin, I'll kill you, you know I can," I threaten.

He wipes away the tears in his eyes from laughing so hard. "You can, but you won't."

He strolls away, and I know full well the whole room is going to know about this within about two minutes.

"Justin," I warn him.

"What month are you, bro?"

"July," Ryan says when I don't answer and Justin bursts out laughing all over again.

I turn my glare on the photographer whose neck I'm about to snap.

He holds up his free hand in surrender. "C'mon, man, it's for charity, and they were going to find out eventually."

I don't even blink, and he pales slightly.

"I think you're going to be the irresistible fighter or something like that. That sounds good, right?" he asks, as he takes a few steps backwards.

I hear laughter across the room and see Rusty and Beast both doubled over.

Pricks. Every last one of them.

"Take it off!" Rusty calls to me, and I flip him off.

I glance across the room and see Ramsey leaning against the wall, an amused expression on her face.

"Don't you start," I warn her.

Her grin grows.

"*Pinky.*"

She giggles, and I crack, a chuckle escaping my lips.

That woman, she's my damn kryptonite.

OTHER TITLES

Love like Yours Series
Rushed – Book 1
Pierced – Book 2
Hunted – Book 3
Chased – Book 4

Rock Games Novels
Paper, Scissors, Rock: Vol. 1
Hide and Seek: Vol. 2

My Heart Duet
My Heart Needs
My Heart Wants

Calendar Boys Novels
Mr. January
Mr. February
Mr. March
Mr. April
Mr. May
Mr. June
Mr. July

ACKNOWLEDGEMENTS

The songs that inspired this book – *Closer* – Kings of Leon, *I'm on Fire* – The Starves and *Walk Me Home* – P!nk.

Hudson and Ramsey's story just flew out of me, and I hope you enjoyed reading it as much as I loved writing it.

I'm not going to lie, after writing this many books in the past few months, I'm running out of new ways to say thank you to the people who help me out so often, so thank you all and please refer to the last book for something more specific lol.

I can't wait for Mr. August!

ABOUT THE AUTHOR

NICOLE S. GOODIN is a romance author and mother of two from Taranaki in the North Island of New Zealand.

In mid-2015, she started to write about a group of characters who wouldn't get out of her head. Her first book, Rushed, was published in mid-2016.

Nicole enjoys long walks on the beach, pillow fights and braiding her friends' hair. She dislikes clichés, talking about herself in the third person, and people who don't understand her sense of humour.

Please feel free to contact her either via her website, email, Instagram, Twitter or on her Facebook page, she would love to hear your feedback. If you're feeling really game, you can even sign up for her newsletter.

Visit www.nicolegoodinauthor.com for more information.

UPCOMING TITLES

Calendar Boys Novels

Mr. August
Mr. September
Mr. October
Mr. November
Mr. December